THE RED EAGLE

A WESTERN TRIO

*Other Five Star Western Titles
by Ray Hogan:*

Soldier in Buckskin
Legend of a Bad Man
Guns of Freedom
Stonebreaker's Ridge

THE RED EAGLE

A WESTERN TRIO

RAY HOGAN

Five Star
Unity, Maine

Five Star First Edition Western Series.

Published in 2001 in conjunction with
Golden West Literary Agency

Set in 11 pt. Plantin by Minnie B. Raven.

Printed in the United States on permanent paper.

Library of Congress Cataloging-in-Publication Data

Hogan, Ray, 1908–   T   94173
    The red eagle : a western trio / by Ray Hogan.—1st ed.
        p. cm.
    Contents: Lost brother—A man called America Jones—
    The red eagle.
    ISBN 0-7862-2394-4 (hc : alk. paper)
    1. Western stories. I. Title.
PS3558.O3473 R39 2001
    813′.54—dc21   00-057800

TABLE OF CONTENTS

LOST BROTHER

It was on the fourth day out of the Upper Crossing of the Arkansas River that Aaron Brocaw knew for sure Indians were in the offing. He had risen that particular spring morning with the feel of it in his bones, and after thirty long winters and summers on the frontier a man learned to trust such forewarnings. Impatiently he urged DeProue, Scanlon, and the others with him into movement, barking irritably at the teamsters to get their heavily loaded freight wagons to rolling.

"What's wrong?" DeProue asked in that precise, irritating manner of his.

Brocaw wagged his grizzled head. "By tanny, they's redskins skulking hereabouts! I can smell 'em."

He sat loosely on his little pony, hunched forward in the saddle, trailing the tag rope to his pack mule while he waited for the freighters to start. His faded eyes traveled restlessly over the low hills to the east, prying into the likely ravines, scanning the rims and ridges, digging along the swales. Time after time he came back to the stream, the Picketwire—the Purgatoire, if you were a Frenchy—and examined every foot of scrubby growth along its banks.

"We should have stayed on the main wagon trail," DeProue said then in a dry, dissatisfied voice. It was the third or fourth time he had made the observation since they had entered the low, rolling country far east of the mountains.

Anger plucked at the edges of Brocaw's long mouth. He did not turn, but his words were sharp. "And run into 'Rapahoes for certain! They been raiding and lifting hair along that trail for dang' nigh a month!"

"We could have got through," DeProue said, quietly insistent. He patted significantly the bright metal pistol thrust into his waistband. It was Sam Colt's latest invention, a rapid-fire revolver capable of throwing five bullets as fast as a man could pull the trigger. Each of the three guards and the teamsters was also equipped with one. "Indians haven't run up against these little beauties yet!"

The mountain man glanced over his shoulder. The wagons were ready at last to roll. The lead teamster, an ancient, leathery scrap of a man with pinpoint blue eyes and a straggling mustache, named Hollis, was gathering up his reins. He lifted his right hand in signal. The bitter-faced guard, Scanlon, and the others ranged in alongside, shouting at the mules. The animals threw themselves forward in the harness, and the big wheels of the Murphy wagons began to turn.

"Them little beauties," Brocaw said then, "likely will get more hair lifted in this country than all the raiding the renegades has ever done!"

"That's where you're wrong, old man," the merchant replied. "White men, armed with pistols like I'm bringing into this country, will be able to tame and control the Indians. They'll be no match for the whites once these revolvers are in use."

Brocaw snorted. "I reckon that's what the first man with a rifle figured. And what did it get him? Nothing but a lot of troubles."

"Revolvers are a different thing," DeProue said. He was a tall man, thin and sharp with dark eyes and hair and a quick, excitable nature. From St. Louis, he had said. He was striking West to set up a trading post and make his fortune. He had chosen the rich but dangerous Turquoise Rock country, and, when Aaron Brocaw, upon hearing that bit of information, had stared at him in disbelief, he had said: "I'll arm every white man with a rapid-fire gun. That, with his rifle, will make him like a small army. The Indians will learn to leave us strictly alone."

"And you'll start the dangedest uprisin' you ever heard of along with it," Brocaw observed.

He was remembering that conversation with the merchant that morning as he rode on ahead of the wagons. The tribes were mostly friendly except for an occasional war party of young bucks out proving their manhood. But you had trouble with some whites, too. There were bad ones in all races. On the whole, however, the trails were safe, made so by careful and painstaking efforts on the part of the mountain men and decent traders who realized it was better to get along with the red men than try to trample them underfoot. There were too many of them for that, too few whites, and rapid-fire gun or no the scattered settlers wouldn't stand a chance once the Indians got fired up and took it in mind to drive them out of the country.

And something like the pistols DeProue was bringing into the Turquoise Rock land was the very thing that could do just that. If he had known that was what DeProue had in mind, if he had known about that wooden case of pistols stowed away in the lead wagon, he'd never have agreed to take the party through! He would have let them set there at the Upper Crossing until the wagon tongues rotted and fell off! Any fool deliberately starting off to stir up the country and set it afire ought be staked to an ant hill before he got a wheel turning.

But he hadn't known about it until they were four days under way. And then there wasn't anything he could do about it. He was duty-bound to stay with the party; he just couldn't ride off and leave them, a bunch of greenhorns, to fend for themselves in the vast emptiness of the Utah Territory. That would be murder. But he had let DeProue know what he thought about the pistols. And when the merchant broke open the box and passed one around with a supply of ammunition to each man, he flatly refused to accept one.

And so there was an existing difference between guide and party, a bristling sort of armed truce—and a fond hope on the part of Aaron Brocaw that no parties of Indians would be crossed, friendly or otherwise. The attitude of DeProue and his men, now armed with the rapid-fire handgun, was one of arrogant insolence; they were fairly aching to try out their weapons on some coppery hides.

Thus he kept the short train fairly close to the stream, feeling there was less chance of encounter there. And, if they were attacked, there would be some small advantage in the brush. The valley began to warm with the rising sun, and the night's coolness faded away, taking with it the sparkling dew tipping the grass. Mentally he calculated how much farther he would have to stay with the party. Still a good sixty miles to the Pass. Then a hundred and seventy-five or so then to Santa Fé. A long time yet.

DeProue rode up on his bay gelding. He wore expensive broadcloth and a wide, white hat. The rapid-fire pistol was tucked under his belt, gleaming dully in the sunlight. Brocaw glanced to it, his lip curling slightly at the sight of the small bit of iron that posed such a threat to him and all others on the frontier.

"You be mighty careful with that gun," he said to the merchant. "Don't you be using it 'less'n I tell you. Likely we'll be crossing trails with some friendlies, and I don't want them getting any ideas."

"You just get us through," DeProue said coolly. "We'll handle any Indians that show up."

Brocaw clucked his distrust and swung away from the

merchant. Morning ran on into the later hours, and near noon, having seen nothing tangible to bolster his feelings of imminent trouble, Brocaw called a halt in a scatter of small trees near the Purgatoire to rest the mules and horses and eat a light lunch. It was a quiet meal, the mountain man keeping to himself while DeProue and the others lounged in the shade of the wagons. Quite unexpectedly, the guard leader, Scanlon, seeing a ground squirrel along the bank of the stream, drew his revolver and placed two quick shots at the animal. The flat sounds lifted and rolled out across the valley, touching the deep corners of the draws completely and laying echoes through the midday quiet. Brocaw was on his feet instantly, padding swiftly to where the guard sat.

"You heard me say they was to be no shooting while we crossed the flats!" he snapped. "Up the way maybe it was all right. Down here it's something else. Now, every redskin in the country knows just where we're nooning."

Scanlon laid his humorless eyes on Brocaw. There was a cocked, coiled quality to the dark man that marked him immediately. Brocaw had seen his type before, often, in saloons and in the trading posts and forts up and down the line. Men with ever-glowing tempers, too quick with their trigger fingers and completely thoughtless of others and their future. But they were hard, brave men who lived recklessly on danger.

Scanlon said: "Simmer down, old man. Indians are not going to bother us."

"Anyway," DeProue broke in, "we can take care of ourselves, if they do."

"Maybe we can, and maybe we can't," Brocaw replied. "Besides, you ain't rememberin' you're not the only people in this country."

"So?" Scanlon pressed.

Brocaw stared at the guard's insolent face. He had an urge to use his long knife, and fifteen years ago it was likely he would have. Scanlon was the kind who brought trouble down on others, a violation of the unwritten law all frontier settlers observed. But it would do no good now. The swift anger ebbed. He turned to the merchant.

"Not again am I telling you this, DeProue. Either we do this my way or you go it alone."

"Let the old man go," Scanlon murmured.

But DeProue had other thoughts. He got to his feet. "Now, hold on, Brocaw. No need to go flying off the handle. I want to get these wagons through, and, if I'd figured to do it alone, I'd never have hired you in the first place. I can't have you quit me now."

"Then be listening to what I tell you and doing what I say. Either I boss this train, or I don't."

Silence dropped over the group broken only by the muted sounds of the stock feeding on the short grass and the harsh chirps of a bird down the stream.

"You're paying him to guide this train," Hollis the teamster drawled from beneath his wagon. "Why don't you let him do it?"

"I am," DeProue insisted. "We have a few differences, but he's running this outfit. I want everybody to understand that."

Brocaw didn't wait to hear any comments. He turned back to his horse and swung to the saddle. For a long time he sat quietly, letting his thoughts run their course. He wished he could feel better about things and that he could shake the disturbed, worried nagging at his mind. But there was no getting away from it. Hearing the wagons groan into movement, he urged his pony forward.

A herd of a half hundred antelope raced away to the south,

their white rumps flashing like signal flags in the bright sunlight. Redskins close by? Brocaw considered that, as the undulating ribbon of white hurried off into the distance. He continued to watch for a time, and then tension within him relaxed. Evidently his party had been the one that had frightened the pronghorns.

The valley deepened soon after that, and near the middle of the afternoon the butte country broke into sight, running low and red-faced to their left. It was not extensive but of great roughness in direct contrast to the rolling hills and flat land. Around five o'clock they reached the first outcroppings, and there Brocaw saw proof of his hunch. Even as he flung his sharp glance toward a faint movement in the breaks, an Indian flashed across a gully.

He made no announcement of this to the others but veered the train slowly for the crest of a small rim. Hot prickles began to run up his spine, and a sudden, heavy breathlessness seemed to settle down over the valley, narrow at this point. He had the sensation of being trapped in the narrow end of a funnel. There was no way of telling if the Indians were friendly or otherwise, and so, when the top of the knob was reached, he signaled for a halt.

DeProue and Scanlon rose up quickly. The merchant said: "What the hell you stopping here for? It's too early for a camp."

Brocaw's eyes were on the buttes. He said calmly: "Redskins." At that same moment he caught the briefest sight of color as the sun caught up and touched the rump of a spotted pony racing across an opening.

Scanlon spat. "Where's any redskins? I sure don't see none."

"You won't," Brocaw replied dryly. "You won't see them till they're ready for you to. But they're out there."

13

"How many?" Scanlon went on, disbelief riding his tone.

Brocaw shrugged. "You guess. Maybe ten. Maybe twenty. Maybe fifty or a hundred. That ain't bothering me right now. I'd like to know what bunch they are, and what's on their mind."

This was Arapahoe country, but it could be Osages out hunting since they still claimed all the territory from the Missouri to the Rocky Mountains as their own. They continually warred with the other tribes over it. Or they might be Eutaws down from the north or Kiowas from the south and east.

DeProue began to show nervousness. "Well, what do we do?"

Brocaw faced the merchant. Light breeze ruffled his long beard and stirred the fringes of his buckskins. His mouth was a straight, gray slash, and the frostiness of his eyes reached out and touched each of the men.

"Just this. We're in trouble for sure, if this is a war party. Could get our hair lifted quick. Don't none of you do anything foolish. You just set quiet like and leave me do the palaverin' if they come to talk."

Scanlon spat contemptuously. "Let 'em come. With these rapid-fire guns we'll handle them."

There it was, the thing Brocaw feared most of all. The fools seemed to think these were the only Indians in the whole blamed country. His eyes narrow, he said: "You make a move to use that thing and I'll blow you out of the saddle! Goes for every man jack of you!"

Turning then, he motioned DeProue to follow. They rode off the low hill onto the narrow strip of flats that lay between them and the buttes. Bidding the merchant to stand, Brocaw continued on, riding in a wide circle several times, the universal sign language request for a parley. It was in his mind to bring the Indians out before dark, to see what their intentions were, if possible. After a few minutes repeating the maneuver, he returned to the merchant.

Time dragged. The sun dropped lower toward the rim of hills to the west. The air in the valley remained hot, however, and filled with a tense stillness. Insects clacked in the grass, and somewhere along the Purgatoire a beaver slapped noisily. One of the mules, aggravated by a deerfly or such similar nuisance, shook himself violently, and the clatter of harness metal drifted out over the way. Overhead the blue brilliance of the cloudless sky was like a vast, inverted bowl. Brocaw grunted a warning. Coming from the buttes was a full-bonneted chief on a wiry, spotted pony. He was closely trailed by three braves.

"*Humph!*" The word escaped DeProue. "That all there is to your Indian party?"

The mountain man shook his head. "Look sharp along the ridge. Reckon you'll spot aplenty more."

Brocaw kept his eyes on the approaching Indians. The first one, the old one, was a full war chief. The brave just behind him was a two-feather chief, judging from the plumes thrust into his headband. The others were warriors. They carried flintlock Hawken rifles across their laps, and, when they had drawn close, he recognized them as Osages. They had that peculiar elongated head appearance, a result of an old tribal custom that bound infants tightly to their cradleboard. He was some relieved to know they were not Eutaws or Arapahoes.

"Osages," he said then, passing the information on to DeProue. "That there first old chief is White Buffalo. Just stay put 'less'n I call you."

He swung from the saddle and, hand upraised, walked slowly forward. The Indians stopped. White Buffalo and the junior chief dismounted and advanced gravely to meet him. A

15

scant yard they paused, and for a full, tense minute the man of the mountains and the Osage warriors looked each other over with studious care.

"Greetings, my brother, White Buffalo. Strong chief of the great Osage people," Brocaw began, employing his customary flourish of words so dear to the tribes. His mastery of the dialect with its complementing sign language was complete, and he saw with a deal of satisfaction the interest break in the chief's hard, beady eyes. "It has been long since I sat with you around your council fires."

White Buffalo's gaze was a piercing, direct shaft. His face was stiff as dry cowhide. "I know you not as my brother, old man."

Brocaw shrugged disdainfully. He had hoped the Osage chief would remember him, but he must not show his disappointment. "My brother has a short memory, for it is so. I am as somebody you have lost but have now found. But tell me why do the brave Osages hide in the hills like coyotes? Three days have I known you were there. Do you fear the white men?"

It was bold, dangerous talk, but Aaron Brocaw knew the nature of the red man and the trails their minds would follow. He knew he must grasp the situation first within his own hands and press the advantage ruthlessly. He must never show, at any moment, the slightest uncertainty or fear. He waited, knowing the answer that would come.

"The Osage people fear nothing!"

The young sub-chief stepped forward, words lifting explosively from his lips. He made a gesture at his mouth and rubbed his palms together angrily. It meant literally: *We have talked too much. We must rub them out.*

White Buffalo watched stonily. He made no reply. To Brocaw he said finally: "We want presents. We want guns.

Tobacco. We want the gun that shoots many times from the hand."

It came to the mountain man then why the Osage party had been hesitant to attack. They had witnessed the target practice sessions with the rapid-fire revolver back up the trail. The mystery of it had deterred them, making them unsure of their abilities despite their superior numbers. He felt his hopes rise. If he could keep White Buffalo uncertain, believing they would fight if pressed and still hold DeProue and his guards in hand, there was a good chance they could get by this war party without bloodshed.

"Where are your peltries trade for guns?" he asked. "I see no buffalo robes. Guns are for trading. We will give you presents but no more."

Two Feathers muttered again, but White Buffalo stilled him with a wave of his brown arm. "You travel in the land of the Osages. You will do as I, their chief, will say!"

Brocaw shook his head. "We are in the land of the 'Rapahoes, enemy of the Osages. We harm neither tribe. We are friends to both. We ask only to cross the trails in peace. You know me as a brother who speaks not with false tongue."

"I remember you not from other times," White Buffalo said doggedly.

Time, a thin, explosive thing, wore on. The mules and horses stamped impatiently. DeProue squirmed in the saddle, and Scanlon, his voice riding plainly through the quiet, swore in a steady, monotonous line. But this was the way of things; each faction stated its thoughts, its ideas, its claims and purposes. It was the time for parley. Violence, if necessary, would come later.

"You remember not when I was a young boy and came to live with you and your people on the banks of the mighty river called the Missouri? I grew tall with your sons. I hunted the

17

buffalo on the plains and ate the raw liver and gall with you at your feasts. I have never had a forked tongue, White Buffalo, and I speak truly. We mean you and your people no harm. Nor will we live on your hunting ground. We ask only to cross and reach the land far to the setting of the sun. As your brother, I tell you these things in truth."

White Buffalo stared at Brocaw steadily. After a time he shook his head. "The moons are many. I remember you not as my brother. You are of the white people, not of the great Osage tribe. We have found you on our land. Now you must pay with many presents."

Brocaw took his first full breath. There was no mention of guns now in the demands of the chief, proving White Buffalo recognized the fact he was not in a good bargaining position. Presents, yes, that was customary and to be expected. But guns were something that must be traded for. He turned and motioned to DeProue.

"They'll let us pass without trouble if we give them presents. Break out some beads and cloth and a few mirrors. They've forgotten about wanting guns now."

DeProue raised his eyes to White Buffalo, a frown drawing up his narrow face. He had understood little of the conversation, of course, but the request was something he could comprehend, and it provoked him. He turned angry. There was no understanding in him for the necessity of paying such tribute, and it showed in the deep flesh that spread up his neck and over his face.

"Why, now . . . that's a devil of a note!" he exclaimed. "Why the hell should I give these savages anything?"

Brocaw swung to face him fully. "You're sure wanting trouble!"

This was the moment he had feared. This was that critical time when the tree would fall one way or the other, and there would be peace or there would be bloodshed. That DeProue's well-armed men could probably handle the Osage party was fairly certain, but that would be only the beginning. It was still a long way to the Turquoise country, and not for time to come, if ever, would the trails be safe for other travelers. The word would spread quickly, and not only would the Osages ever after be thirsting for vengeance but all the other tribes as well, since they would expect similar treatment at the hands of all white men.

"It's the usual thing," he said then, trying to remain cool. "Don't cost you much, and it's better'n blood spilling."

DeProue flung a glance to Scanlon and his other men. For a moment he seemed to consider while the silence ran on in measured, throbbing beats. Suddenly he came to conclusion; he drew his pistol and kicked his horse into plunging forward motion.

"The devil with it!" he yelled, and drove hard for White Buffalo.

Brocaw's long rifle rapped its sound across the immediate confusion. DeProue swayed in the saddle and fell heavily to the ground as the ball smashed into his shoulder. Brocaw scooped up the man's fallen pistol and faced Scanlon and the others, starting to surge forward.

"Nobody move," he snapped, "unless you're wanting to die!"

Behind him he heard the rapid pound of horses as White Buffalo and his warriors rushed back for the buttes and the rest of the braves. The thought came to him: *Now they'll sure come swooping down on us!* He waited until the sound had died and then strode to where DeProue lay moaning softly on the grass.

"You're a plain fool!" he said. "Now we'll be lucky if we reach the Pass with our hair."

19

The merchant struggled to a sitting position. Blood stained down the front of his shirt, and he mopped at the wound with a yellowed handkerchief. "You'll answer for this!" he gritted. "I'll see to that!"

"Better get to the settlement alive first," Brocaw said easily. "You're a mighty far place from there now."

Scanlon came up and helped the merchant to his feet. DeProue ducked his head at Brocaw. "Take these guns away from him and tie his hands so he can't get away."

"How you figure to reach the Pass?" Brocaw asked dryly.

"We'll get there," the merchant replied. "Don't worry about that. All we have to do is follow out this stream. One of you men come over here and fix up my arm."

The mountain man smiled. "Following out the old Picketwire will land you smack dab up against the Sangre de Cristo Mountains."

Silence dropped over the group, each man considering the bald possibilities. Hollis the teamster was the first to speak. "Man could ride forever in this country and get no place. You sure got to know where you're headed."

"Now, I'll tell you what," Brocaw said then. His tone was sharp. "I'm sick of this outfit. I'll take you to the Pass and drop you there. You can set on your haunches till somebody else comes along that'll take you on through. That's agreeable so long as they's no more talk about taking my guns and tying up my hands. Otherwise, I'm climbing aboard my horse and moving out right now."

"Try that," Scanlon said softly, "and I'll blow your head off!"

"Then what would you do? You'd sure be in a predicament!"

"He's right there," Hollis murmured.

DeProue flicked a glance to Scanlon who stared back at

him for a moment, and then smiled. "All right," the merchant said. "It's a deal. You take us to the settlement at the Pass. We'll be on our own after that."

Brocaw turned for his horse. The cunning look passed between the merchant and his chief guard had not escaped his sharp eyes. Already he was studying about it, figuring what they had in mind.

"What about them Indians?" Hollis asked.

"We'll keep moving on till near dark," Brocaw replied without halting. "I'm hoping they kept going."

But he had his doubts about that. White Buffalo, his pride injured and goaded on by Two Feathers, would more than likely return in full force. DeProue had pulled a foul stunt, one that could cost them all their lives. But there was no use thinking of that. The damage was done. If the Osage party struck, there would be nothing left to do but fight—and with the rapid-fire pistols DeProue proposed to tame all the tribes with but which would, in the end, start a conflagration that would envelop the whole frontier. Brocaw swore softly. One thing was certain: if they did get through without a fight, he was going to do something about those pistols!

They made good time, despite the wounded DeProue. Evening of the fifth day they made camp at the foot of the mountains, only a half day from the settlement at the Pass. DeProue, in better spirits despite his lame arm, broke out a gallon jug of brandy, and they all gathered around the fire to celebrate the completion of the journey's second leg. They had seen no further signs of the Osage war party, and this, because he could not understand it, disturbed Aaron Brocaw considerably. But he doubted now if they would attack. They were too close to the settlement.

Scanlon and his two guards were soon very drunk. With

the exception of Hollis, the teamsters were not far behind them, and by midnight all but the wagon driver and Brocaw were dead to the world.

"Reckon I'll stand watch for a spell," the mountain man said to Hollis. "Don't pay to forget them Indians."

The teamster nodded, tossing more wood into the dying fire. "I'll get forty winks and then stand my share," he said. "Call me when you're ready."

Brocaw said—"Fair enough."—and moved off to a low hill a few yards distant from the camp.

The night was bright, flooded by the moon and strong, silver star shine. The prairies rolled away eastward in soft, rounded waves, and the towering mountains, to the west and north and south, were dark, overhanging curtains. Somewhere back in the cañons a wolf howled. Brocaw was instantly alert, but when no answer came, he settled back down, turning his eyes toward the camp.

He watched Hollis crawl into his blankets, thrash about until he found comfortable rest, and go quiet with sleep. The fire was blazing brightly, and Brocaw held his position for a full hour, until he was certain all were sleeping soundly and the flames had dwindled. Then, moving silently as a soaring eagle, he slipped into the camp. He went immediately to the lead wagon, located the small case of rapid-fire pistols, and carried it to the edge of the clearing.

He returned almost immediately and slunk among the sleeping men. He found all of the pistols that had been issued by DeProue, except the one carried by Scanlon, and unloaded them. Scanlon's he would have to forget. He couldn't risk awakening the man. He tossed the ammunition into the brush and went again to the wagon. From it he took a second box, one containing the extra supply of ammunition, and this he carried to the clearing's limits. An hour later the pistols and the box of bullets and other equipment were lying on the bottom of a deep pool beneath a waterfall a half mile north of the camp. When that was done, he awakened Hollis, and took his turn in the blankets. He felt much better about the future.

DeProue had Brocaw arrested immediately when arriving at the Pass and before he could effect the escape he had planned. The charge was attempted murder. The merchant had not discovered the loss of his rapid-firing pistols, but, wanting to put on a demonstration for the inhabitants of the settlement, he found that out when they went to the wagon.

DeProue was near insane with rage. He tried everything from cajolery to brutality on the old mountain man to no avail, and, when darkness fell, Aaron Brocaw sat in the soddy jail well-satisfied. There was to be a court trial the following morning. The result was a foregone conclusion: he had no illusions, knowing full well the influence a merchant such as DeProue would have in a small settlement like the Pass. He worried little about it. If it was meant for him to die at the end of a hanging rope, then that was the way he would die. One thing was good: there would be no man like Scanlon walking around with rapid-fire pistols to start trouble on the frontier. That was worth hanging for.

Sometime after dawn the marshal, gun in hand, brought him a plate of bacon and corn cakes and a tin cup of black coffee. Brocaw ate unhurriedly, and, when he was finished, he stood at the single, small window looking out over the long sweep of valley land. It was pretty hard for a man to leave country such as this.

He had planned to trap the Purgatoire that coming season, after September when the furs got right. He had heard it was good country, and, while he doubted he could, anywhere, nearly touch the thousand dollars' worth of prime peltries he had taken that last winter along the Red River and the Washita, it would be good to try. Anyway, he could always drop back over the pass into the Culebras, north of Taos, if it didn't work out. He shrugged. He guessed there wasn't much use of thinking about it now.

His thoughts moved to Taos where he usually spent the summer months. He had a wife there, a Spanish woman, and he hadn't seen her for better than a year. She would be looking for him and wondering why he didn't show up. But somebody would carry the news on to her. She'd feel right bad about it. And so would St. Vrain and Carson, when they heard.

He stepped back then, hearing footsteps approach. He waited quietly as the marshal unlocked the door. Not all of the fight was gone from him yet, and he watched the man narrowly, searching for some means of escape. But the lawman's gun was a steady threat, and he walked out into the fall sunlight, shading his eyes from the glare, as he was directed. Moving ahead of the marshal, he crossed the narrow street and entered a small courtroom where two dozen or so people stood against a back wall facing a florid-cheeked man who sat behind a low table. DeProue, his shoulder in bandages, and Scanlon were at a long bench at one side. The marshal escorted him to a chair opposite and directed him to sit.

The judge cleared his throat. "Marshal, see's there is no guns in this courtroom."

The officer made his examination, finding one or two that he laid in a corner near several chairs. He then took up a position just inside the doorway. A hush fell over the room, and Brocaw, feeling some of the tenseness creep into his own body, let his gaze drift out over the gathering, seeing much, seeing nothing. But he did note the redness of the judge's countenance and the sagging eyelids, and in him recognized a drunkard. Heat had begun to rise within the place, and sunlight reached in through the door, spreading an oblong block upon the pine flooring.

"You, the defendant, Brocaw," the judge began in a dragging voice, "are accused by a Henry DeProue of attempted murder. You guilty or not?"

The stillness hung. After a short time Brocaw said: "If you mean did I shoot him, I sure did."

"You are guilty of the charge, then?"

The old mountain man looked through the doorway. He shrugged. "Had I wanted to kill him, I would have done that. I was just stopping him."

"But you admit you did shoot the aforementioned Henry DeProue. Therefore, you are guilty as charged."

DeProue got to his feet. "Your honor," he said with great elaborateness, "I am prepared to drop this charge under certain conditions."

The judge swung his hazy eyes at the merchant. "I'm not sure a murder charge can be dropped. What have you got on your mind?"

"A quite valuable shipment was removed from one of my wagons by the defendant. If he will tell me where he hid it, I will withdraw my charge."

The judge swiveled his gaze to Brocaw. "You heard the complainant. What do you say?"

Brocaw's eyes were still on the world beyond the open doorway. He could hear birds singing and the gentle rustle of the breeze slipping through the cottonwoods. The hills were a dull gray-green haze, looking cool and inviting and filled with promise. So far away at the moment. He shook his head. It would be nice to be free and tramp the hills and valleys again, but he guessed he'd had his share of that. He wasn't young any more, and maybe what he was doing would make it safe

25

for others, for those younger to do what he had done.

"I reckon not," he said.

There was a sudden, excited scuff of boots among the audience as the judge's voice droned: "It becomes my duty as judge to sentence you to hang for attempting to kill one of your fellow men. Said sentence to take place right now at the big tree on the north end of town.''

There was a rush for the door as people surged to get a good position from which to watch. The marshal trod up soberly and, touching Brocaw on the shoulder, got him to his feet. Tying his wrists behind him, he led him outside and helped him into the saddle of his pony, after which he walked him the short distance to where the crowd had gathered. A rope already dangled from the cottonwood's lowest limb, which showed scarred evidence of such previous use. The marshal came to a halt there and, reaching up, adjusted the noose around the old mountain man's scrawny neck.

"Anything you want to say?" he asked.

Brocaw looked out over the crowd. He saw DeProue and Scanlon standing to one side, question still in the merchant's eyes. He turned deliberately away and laid his eyes upon the green of the valley, toward the Spanish Peaks far to the left. Beyond them were the shadowy outlines of the taller hills. He trembled a little, the thought of hanging setting up its natural revulsion within him. He hadn't expected to leave life this way. He had figured it would come with an arrow, a rifle ball, or maybe a tomahawk in the hands of some skulking Eutaw. Not this way. Not by hanging. But a man just couldn't figure some things. He shook his head and lowered his eyes to the ground.

Expectancy fell over the gathering, laying its restraint upon all sounds. And then a voice, strangled and hollow in its consistency and fear, gasped: "Indians!"

An arrow swished through the stillness. It *thunked* solidly into the cottonwood's rough trunk. Brocaw, suddenly aware of the interruption, lifted his gaze wonderingly. A solid ring of painted Osage warriors surrounded the crowd. They sat their ponies silently, some with rifles, others with drawn bows and arrows ready in their muscular hands. The ring parted, and White Buffalo rode forward. He drew a long-bladed knife from his woven belt and severed the rope looped around Brocaw's neck and also the one that bound his wrists.

His hard, beady eyes met those of the mountain man, and for a moment a softness altered them. "I remember, lost brother," he said gravely. "Come."

Wheeling, the Osage chief rode back into the ranks of his warriors with Aaron Brocaw close behind.

A MAN CALLED AMERICA JONES

It took thirty years, thirty long, inflexible years, but now I can walk to the big, wide bay window of the old house, look out upon the burnished fields of good ripe grain, and fully understand the entity that was America Jones.

There were many things that at one time disturbed me: was he actually a man afraid, a coward? Why was he one eternally apart, never mingling with other men of the valley, who, instead, stood alone, cool and aloof, like an invincible pillar of upthrusting rock on a steep hillside? And why was he a man of many acquaintances but actually had none who took him as a genuine friend? Too late I now realize that the steadfast calmness that lay upon him like a thick blanket was no more than just that, a thin veneer under which existed sultry, banked fires capable of flaring into blazing life. Only today have the pieces of that confused puzzle fallen into place, and I am the lost child stepping suddenly from the blackest cavern into the pure light of full revelation.

When America Jones arrived at the head of the lush Truchas Valley country the War Between the States was five years behind him. The memories of Lee and Malvern's Hill and bloody Antietam—and that affair at Proctor's Hill—were fading into the dark shadows of the past. But they had left their deep and powerful scars. Violence was forevermore no part of him.

He came alone, and the journey had been long and lonely. Myra, his bride, remained with his parents in the States, waiting until he could get the homestead under way, after which he would send for her. He brought only the wagon in which he rode, drawn by a team of strong, black mules, and the few, pitiful belongings that were their sole possessions. With those things and the strength of his big hands he would carve a future from this wild, frontier land.

He stood, that early spring day, on the brow of the hill overlooking the north end of the valley and pointed out his holdings to squat Hugo Schultz, the storekeeper at the settlement of Sentinel, fifteen miles or so to the south. He wasn't a big man, this America Jones, but he stood a full head and shoulders above the merchant, and, as he spoke, the cool gravity of his eyes fled momentarily, and a spark glowed, stirred by some inner excitement, and the grim lines of his face relaxed slightly.

"The tall posts mark the corners of my land. There is a good spring, over there where that stand of cottonwoods is. I will always have water, come dry summer or a wet one. The soil is rich, and things will grow. I would ask your favor for seeds and groceries until I can get a crop out."

Perhaps it was the look on Jones's face, or possibly the way he spoke the words *my land* and the manner in which they left his lips as if they were reverent, hallowed words, but Schultz did something he had vowed long ago never to do again. He said, speaking in that careful, precise fashion of the foreign-born who had painstakingly learned a difficult tongue: "I am willing that it should be so. You have credit for your seeds."

America Jones turned slowly to the man. There was no smile on his face, but there was in his eyes, in his words. "You have my thanks. It is a thing you'll never regret."

Thus it began. With only the ten-foot poles set deeply into the earth to go by, he went doggedly about the back-breaking task of working up the soil and preparing it for a crop. He lived out of his wagon and, during the evening hours, built the sod shanty that was to be his and Myra's first home. It was in those hours that he missed her most of all, the long, cool evenings with the dark sky bending closely overhead, lighted by its scatter of sparkling silver stars.

On Sundays he rode one of the mules to the settlement for services, but he made no good friends. The shy reticence of emigrant parents, who had demonstrated their appreciation of the country that had received them so kindly by abandoning their own unpronounceable name for that of Jones and by calling their first-born after it, laid its restraint upon him and kept him still and apart while others talked and passed the time of day.

Only Hugo Schultz, no different on Sunday than weekdays, except for the absence of the bibbed apron, had some thought of the man's inner being and could guess at his background. He assumed much from the tattered remainders of the uniform Jones wore, and he read a great deal in the haunted grimness of his face, but he said nothing, neither to Jones nor to any others of the settlement. A man's life was his own. But he had a certain fatherly interest in the matter, and one young day in late fall he said, not inquisitively: "You plan someday you might fence in your place?"

Jones nodded. "It should be done."

"Maybe you should not," the storekeeper said, a slight strand of worry running through his tone. "This mostly is country for cattle. Stockmen will not take kindly to wire strung across the Truchas."

Jones shrugged. "Why should they care? The valley is not theirs. They run their cattle on the flat land back of the rims. If they didn't like a homestead in the valley, they would have said so before now, wire or no wire."

Old Schultz, aware of the minds of men, shook his head sadly. "Now they say nothing. But strung wire will draw their nettles. It is not good."

"Anyway," America Jones said in a tone so cold and flat that the storekeeper raised his glance suddenly, "it is my land. My own. Nobody changes that."

It was a short winter, and spring came winging in on warm rains that drew the crops in fine shape. Late that fall he sent for Myra, forwarding the two hundred dollars railroad and coach fare through Schultz, and set about getting everything in top shape for her appearance. Four days before he was to leave for Williamstown to meet her, a marauding band of Arapaho Indians, far south of their ordinary range, swooped down from the hills and raided the homestead. Failing to fire the sod structures he had built, they contented themselves with breaking up the few pieces of furniture, slashing to ribbons anything of cloth, and cutting down the half dozen young fruit trees he had planted. They ended their foray by driving off one of the mules, the other, by chance, having been with Jones in the lower field at the time.

It was a sickening blow and a terrible loss, but it was too late to stop Myra, and he met her on the appointed day at the station and brought her back, not to the well-started farm he had written about but to a place of shambles.

Stubbornly he began anew with Myra now at his side, the setback seeming less appalling. Luckily the winter again was a mild one, permitting him to labor well into January, and the crops once more were exceptional, and a ready market was found in Sentinel for any portion they wished to sell. They were able to buy many of the much needed things they had gone without, including a good Jersey cow. Late in October their first child, a boy, was born, and then winter, seemingly to take issue with its previous gentleness, laid a solid grasp upon the Truchas country.

Snow piled five feet on the levels, fifteen in the drifts. The cow froze to death, and the horse they had traded a load of corn for met a similar fate. The frost never left the ground until late May, a laggardly introduction to a short, dry summer that produced a thin crop. The cold months came and with them terrible days and nights, hard and bitter, when nothing outside the range of heat and protection could move. A less stubborn man would have called it quits, but not America Jones. Through it all he plodded patiently on, like a mill wheel in an ever-flowing river, complaining little, doing all in his power to lighten the burden on Myra.

"One thing," he said to her in his slow, calm way, as they sat huddled before the fireplace one bitter January night, "we have our troubles, but we have our health." He paused, listening to the cry of the wind as it tore its way through the valley, lashing the trees, sweeping the snow into deep drifts. He added thoughtfully: "And we have our land."

Myra glanced quickly at him, searching his brooding eyes for any sign of that hopelessness that had shadowed him since the day at Proctor's Mill. It had almost vanished since they had come to the Truchas, and now it could return, bringing that desperate, pinched futility she knew so well. But it was not there, and in those moments she was thankful even for the austerity of their life, for the howling of the gale outside, since these things all filled him with other enigmas and left no room for past recollections.

The second baby came late in the spring, arriving in the midst of a whirling snowstorm, and they named her Murelda after Myra's mother. That summer a wildcat killed all the chickens, but good crops made it possible for them not only to replace that loss but buy another cow, a horse, and afford the many other things they so direly needed, and America Jones began to think of a new house to replace the soddy, larger and better and trimmed with wood as all fine houses should be.

That next year was best of all. Things grew in the valley beyond all expectations, and at the outset of winter they had purchased a team, a good wagon, and enough lumber with which to start building. And there was money for fencing. To cap it all another family of homesteaders moved in some ten miles down the valley, and for the first time they had neighbors of their own kind which pleased Myra mightily.

"Now the children will have someone to play with, and we can go visiting and can go to church together and have socials just like we did back in the States!"

America Jones, holding her close, listened to the words and felt her happiness and saw the beginning of the fulfillment of his dream, and the past slid further away.

That next Saturday was their usual trip to Sentinel for supplies. Myra had shopping to do, and Jones stood in the coolness of Schultz's store after loading the wagon, passing the time while waiting. The children ranged behind the counters and in the open spaces, exhausting their curiosity of all the wonderful things the shelves held.

"It has been a good year," Schultz said, replacing the dry brick in the tobacco case with one that had been soaked, as a moistening agent.

Jones nodded. "The best."

"Another of this kind and Truchas will be the richest valley in the country," the storekeeper continued. He paused, about to say more, but was checked as a shadow blocked his screened doorway. Jones glanced to the big man entering.

Schultz said: "Come in, Mister Burke. Come in."

Jones nodded a half greeting, and the cattleman moved closer. This was Olin Burke, this big, dark, hard-faced man, half owner of the vast KEY Ranch whose thousands of acres lay across the prairie like the sky itself. With his partner, Clee Davis, he ruled the huge empire with an iron hand.

33

"The rig out front," he began, ignoring the greeting, "the one with the barb wire in it. Whose is it?"

The room suddenly hushed. A tenseness, tangible as steel mesh, caught up the stillness, and the threat in Burke's deep voice laid a heavy pressure upon the others. An older man pushed gently through the door and took up his position behind Burke, murmuring: "Now, Olin, no need for trouble."

"Stay clear of this, Clee," Burke growled, not looking around. "Your outfit?" he said then to Jones.

The homesteader nodded. "Mine."

"You the mucker that strung up some wire at the upper end of the valley? And now you're planning to put up more?"

"It's my land," Jones said. "It needed fencing, and I fenced it."

Burke wagged his head. "You can take it down. I need that water. I'll be moving in a bunch of stock in the next few days, and they'll be grazing right where you're squatting. Best you not be there."

"That's my land," Jones said doggedly. "You can't run your cattle on it."

The breathless silence hung momentarily. Schultz cleared his throat, and Clee Davis stirred uneasily. From the street came the off-key tinkling of the piano in Nixon's Bar. Somewhere a dog barked in slow, spaced monotony.

"Friend," Olin Burke said in a dry voice, "KEY does anything."

The cattleman took a step forward, seized Jones by the shirt front, and threw his huge flat fist into the homesteader's face. Jones sagged against the counter, and a host of small, stacked items clattered to the floor.

"Here now!" Schultz exclaimed protestingly.

Burke dragged Jones upright and again smashed a blow into the man's jaw. The homesteader went to his knees and

34

started to rise again. Both children were screaming by now, and in that moment Myra burst through the doorway. She caught the scene in a single glance, brushed past Burke, and dropped to her knees by her husband.

" 'Merick! 'Merick!" she cried. "What's happening?"

Jones shook his head and got slowly to his feet. Blood trickled from a corner of his crushed lips, and a bluish swelling was lifting beneath one eye. He raised his clouded gaze to Burke, standing tall and proud, appraising Myra with frank and open disapproval.

"It's my land," he restated in a weary voice. "You stay off it."

Burke considered him then, with dry humor. "We'll see, we'll see," he murmured. "But you better take that pretty little wife of yours and those kids and get out of here before somebody gets hurt." Spinning on a heel, he left the store with Clee Davis following silently.

It did not end there. In the stunned silence of the room, broken only by the sobbing of the children, Olin Burke's booming voice came again. "All right, boys, tip 'er over!"

Almost at once there was a crash and the jingling of harness metal. Jones, followed by Myra and Hugo Schultz, hurried to the doorway. Two of KEY's cowboys had tossed loops over the off wheel hubs and tipped the wagon over, spilling its contents into the street to the vast amusement of many onlookers.

Myra's voice, pitched to the breaking point, cried out to Schultz: "Isn't there any law in this country? Where's the marshal? Don't innocent people have any protection against such men as Burke and Davis?"

The old German shook his head sadly. "KEY owns the law, too. Everything is KEY."

"There must be some protection," Myra protested. She

watched America Jones move slowly out onto the porch and start for the capsized wagon.

"A man's his own protection," Schultz said. "Your husband must fight his own way. He must carry his gun and stand up for himself."

"But he won't," Myra said in a stricken voice. "He won't fight. Accidentally he killed his best friend during the war. At a place called Proctor's Mill. He swore he would never again use a gun or raise his hand to fight, and he never has."

Schultz pushed past her, intending to help Jones right the wagon, but the homesteader shook his head. "Would mean only trouble for you," he said. "This is my problem."

Back on the porch Schultz wagged his head again. He watched as Jones placed his shoulder to the side of the light vehicle's bed and forced it back to its four wheels. He spent a minute quieting the team, and then began methodically and deliberately to pick up the scattered items. Of the dozen or more watching, none offered assistance. Nobody bucked KEY. To have offered help would have been considered an admission of sentiment, and there was none, regardless of one's inner feelings, who desired to risk it.

After the wagon had been reloaded, Jones returned to the store. "We are ready to go," he said in a hollow voice.

Myra gathered up the children and started for the door. Schultz said: "You are not safe in this valley from this time on. You are welcome to have my pistol." He ducked his head at the heavy gun lying on a shelf behind the counter.

"There'll be no fighting," Jones said.

"You will move, then?" the storekeeper asked.

America Jones shook his head. "No, we will not move. It is our land, and we'll stay."

"I fear you are in for great trouble," Schultz said, and turned away.

That ride back to the homestead was a quiet one. The children slept, and Myra did not press him with talk, for which he was grateful. Thinking back over the incident, he saw the point of differences between himself and Olin Burke as one of available water to the cattleman's herd. That following morning he took the team and a scoop and, at a place a quarter of a mile before his south fence, hollowed out a section of the stream he made into a wide, although shallow, pond. This, he reasoned, would answer Burke's requirements, and future trouble would thereby be circumvented.

Near noon of that same day he paused in his nailing of a window casement in the wall of the new house and watched a herd of cattle coming into the valley from the west ridge. There appeared to be around three hundred head, hazed along by six or eight riders, and, when they reached the floor of the cañon, two of the horsemen disengaged themselves and cantered up to the homestead. One was Burke; the other a man Jones had never seen before. He climbed down from the bench upon which he was standing and met them in the center of the yard.

The cattleman's face was frozen, and anger pulled at the corners of his eyes. He pulled up close to the homesteader and let his cold glance travel slowly over the man. "You moving?"

Jones shook his head. "No, this is my land, and I'm staying." He heard Myra come out of the soddy and felt her presence as she came in behind him and saw the look in Olin Burke's eyes. "You wanted a place to water. I fixed one. No need for you to come to this spring."

"Maybe there is, maybe there isn't," Burke said dryly. "I said I wanted this land for grazing."

"No grazing here. This ground has all been worked. There's no grass inside my fences."

"That's the hell of it," Burke murmured. "You squatters come in and turn out the grass. Today you plow, tomorrow it goes to weeds, or even dust, when the rains don't come. You ruin this country, you and your kind. One of you might do no harm, but you're like maggots. One starts, and, the first thing you know, the country is crawling with the likes of you."

"You don't need my place," Jones said in a low voice. "Why don't you leave us alone?"

"Get out!" Burke said, suddenly alert and angry with the conversation. "I've put that other bunch of nesters on the run, and I'll take no more of your talk. Be gone by tomorrow night, or I'll be back and clean you out!"

He touched spurs to his horse, and the animal lunged forward, shouldering Jones aside, hard, but the homesteader kept his balance. He watched the two men ride from the yard, feeling Myra's hand steal into his own.

"He doesn't need the water. He doesn't need the land. He just wants us out of here," he said aloud. "It's our land. We won't be run off it . . . we'll stay!"

Somewhere below the corral a meadowlark pealed out its song, oblivious to the brittle clash of men. One of the horses nickered, and a vagrant breeze coming down the valley brought with it the smells of wildflowers and mint.

"What can we do?" Myra said then. "He said the others had gone. We're alone now, 'Merick. Completely alone. What can we do?"

Jones turned away, his big shoulders going limp. For a long time he stared straight at the distant slope of the valley. When he answered, his voice was empty, empty and hollow with hopelessness. "I don't know, Myra. I just don't know."

It was an uneasy night, but the next day he was to remember as one of the finest he had ever seen. The fields lay ripe and ready, the sky bright and clear blue, and about all things there was a mellow, soft calmness. Birds trilled in the cottonwoods and willows near the spring, and the swift rumbling of Truchas Creek was a muted song in the still air. The new house was well-started, and chances were they would move in before cold weather really set in—if such was to be. Myra worked inside the soddy at her household tasks, and the children played their noisy games in the sun. But it was false tranquility, Jones knew. Over it all hung the threatening shadow of Olin Burke and KEY.

It was all so simple yet so direly critical. He asked for little: to be left alone with his family, to live his life, harming no one, to work with growing things and feel the good, black soil between his fingers and know the gentle touch of warm rain in the summer. That wasn't asking for much, and yet on this day something stood before him, a towering, monstrous giant, sprung alive and fearful from one man's greed and pride. Olin Burke. Olin Burke. The name revolved in his mind, becoming a curse, a hideous representation of trouble and discouragement, a harbinger of despair and disillusionment. And he was helpless against it. Weary, heartsick, he turned in early, having accomplished little during those daylight hours.

He awakened near midnight, hearing the scatter of gunshots. The pungent odor of smoke filled his nostrils. His first reaction was one of revulsion, and those last moments at Proctor's Mill swept over him when Cal Turrentine's face had risen suddenly and unexpectedly from the brush only to dissolve into a bloody mess when his gun had leaped to life involuntarily as his strained reflexes obeyed their wire-taut master. But the crying of the children and the immediacy of the moment pressed hard upon him, and he came out of the bed and gained the doorway in a single, running step.

A bullet thudded into the wood facing, and he ducked. Outside, the new house was a mass of flames, and beyond it a glare in the lower field told him where other fires were having their destructive way. Myra pulled him down as more bullets drove into the sod walls of the hut, and he lay there trembling, hearing the scream of the horses in the corral and the steady racket of the chickens, cackling their alarm. Riders pounded through the yard, and men's shouting voices filled the night, turned lurid by the glow. Finally, unable to stand the sounds from the suffering livestock any longer, he wrenched free of Myra and started for the barn at a hard run, bullets lacing the path around him.

Near the tool shed he tripped and fell heavily, and, as he arose, half stunned, he heard the riders pulling away toward the hills, the low roll of their horses' hoofs reaching him above the dry crackling of flames. Myra caught up with him, and together they freed the panic-stricken animals, herding them into a small side yard on the north. Most of the chickens were dead as were two of the cows. Luckily the horses were not harmed beyond a little singed hair, but the old mule, the last survivor of America Jones's entry into Truchas Valley, lay near the barn, victim of either a stray, or intended, bullet.

There was nothing they could do for the new house. They stood in the flickering fan of yellow light and watched it burn down to blackened embers, and at dawn, when the first gray streaks rushed down from the hills and revealed the ruin, Myra turned to him with a question.

"What *can* we do?" he answered her, haggard and worn to a knife's edge. The echoes of the gunshots still rocked in his ears, rubbing his nerves to salted rawness, keeping awake the old memories and making him uncertain and distracted. "What's left but to start over again?"

"But we can't go on like this!" Myra said quickly. "We can't start over unless we have help against them. We can't stay and not fight, 'Merick. It's not safe for us any more."

Something inside the man struggled against reason and found voice. "I'll see Davis. I'll see him today. Maybe I can get him to talk to Burke."

"Talking is all so useless," Myra said, turning away. For a moment she hesitated, seemingly about to say more, but the words died on her lips. Her shoulders went limp, and she moved wearily for the soddy. America Jones watched her go, and the great despair within him grew, and all at once he felt cold and very old and tired. He took a step after her, wanting to take her into his arms and assure her that all would come out in the end, that right, after all, was stronger than might, yet a measure of his own pride, of which he now had so little left, caught him up and checked his motion. He would see Davis, and then, perhaps, he could tell her the words that would gladden her heart and take the worry from her mind. At once he hitched up the team and drove to Sentinel.

The cattleman was not at the settlement. Yes, Schultz said, peering at Jones closely, he had seen him earlier in the morning, but he didn't know where he had gone. Burke and several riders had been with him, and they had headed up the valley. Was it not strange he had not passed them on the way? Jones listened to the merchant's words, and a vague uneasiness began to grow within him. Abruptly he wheeled about and started back to his homestead, worry tagging feverishly at his nerves and compelling him to drive the team at a reckless pace. It was something he could not explain to himself, but it was there, a hard core that whipped at him relentlessly, and when, sometime later, he saw three riders outlined on the rim to his left, coming from the north, near frenzy possessed him, and he drove the horses unmercifully. He swirled into the yard at a dead run.

From the house came the wails of the children, but another sound was there, also, the sniffled sobbing of Myra, and he rushed through the doorway, and, finding her crouched against the wall, a terrible wave of horror surged over him. Quickly he gathered her into his arms. She was near hysterics, and it was long moments before she quieted enough to speak.

"He came here . . . Burke did. And some others. Right after you left. He came into the house."

America Jones waited, his face stiff and gray. Dryness filled his mouth. "Were you harmed?" he managed to say.

Myra shook her head weakly. "No . . . but the things he said. Those horrible, vile things . . . and his hands. . . ." She shuddered violently and began to sob again.

All the patient coolness washed from America Jones in that moment. That precluding aversion to violence fled, and a bristling current of anger, white hot in its fierceness, raced through him, and he became that dangerous, unpredictable paradox: a peaceable man filled at last to the brim, finally and wholly aroused.

He placed Myra on the bed and brought the children to her, comforting them as best he could. Afterward, he went outside, saddled a horse, and started for Sentinel at a steady run. He pulled up before Schultz's place, entered, and said to the storekeeper in a level voice: "I will borrow your gun now."

Schultz handed it to him wordlessly, and he turned away. He crossed the street to Nixon's Bar, seeing Burke's gelding at the rail. Schultz shouted something to him, but he didn't hear it. In his mind was a single, straight groove, and down it he walked, unhampered by any past memory, totally oblivious to all else. He mounted the three steps of the porch and pushed through the swinging doors. A dozen or so men, mostly KEY riders, lounged at the bar. Olin Burke, in conversation with Clee Davis, stood near the far end.

"Burke!" Jones called.

Men turned, curiosity fading swiftly from their faces, and

moved hurriedly away. Burke came around, surprise filling his eyes, and Clee Davis stepped away. Burke reached for his gun at his hip, and in that fraction of stilled time America Jones fired. Burke went over backward like a wind-struck fence, his pistol clattering to the floor, his hat rolling drunkenly away. For a brief moment all was confusion. Smoke rolled in small clouds. Men shouted and rushed for the doorway and piled into the street. Voices lifted from the outside, insistent and questioning. In the full, deadly quiet that finally came, Clee Davis said: "I'm sorry about this. I warned him."

"I can leave the valley now," Jones said, and wheeled around.

Looking neither to right nor left along the empty, stilled street, he mounted his horse and returned to the homestead. Myra was standing in the doorway of the soddy when he came up. He stabled the horse and walked woodenly to her.

At the door she stopped him, throwing her arms around him. "Oh, 'Merick . . . I'm so glad you're back! I was so worried."

"Burke's dead," he stated flatly. "He'll never trouble you again."

He stood there, a rigid, uncompromising figure, Myra's arms tightly around him. "It's all over, then," she said after a time.

"Yes, it's all over. Tomorrow we will leave this place."

"Leave!" she echoed. "But why, 'Merick? Burke's gone. KEY will leave us alone now."

"Myra," he said haltingly, "I can't start all over again. I realized back there that I just couldn't do it. It's not in me to begin again."

Myra pulled away from him slightly, the shock of his words and their true meaning reflecting in her eyes the alarm

43

they had lifted within her. A long sigh passed through him. "All the things we hoped to give the children, the good places we made for them, they're gone, Myra. It would take too long now, too long to climb back to yesterday. It's hopeless."

Myra came back into his arms, fighting desperately for him against a totally unfamiliar enemy, one toward which she had but small defenses. "No, 'Merick! It's not hopeless! We can start again! We have ourselves . . . and we still have the land."

He shrugged away and moved to the doorway where he remained, silent, caught up by a sound out there in the night or by some thought passing through him. When he spoke again, his voice was low, and there was little luster to its tone. "I don't know, Myra. I have no heart for it now. I feel . . . well, just angry inside. A man should, in his life, work to leave something for his family, for his children. In that I have failed. There is nothing for them now."

Myra crossed swiftly to his side. "But you have! If nothing else, you will leave them your courage to stand up against the Olin Burkes in this world and the will to go on despite all odds. That's all they will need."

He was a quiet figure in that moment, silhouetted against the star shine of the night, considering her words and letting his emotions have their way with him. A coyote barked into the paleness from the low hills, and somewhere near the spring a beaver slapped a warning to his kind. The softest of breezes drifted up the valley, sweet and friendly, touching all things with its gentleness. He turned then to Myra, the suggestion of a smile across his long lips, and she knew at once that all was well, that he had come back from some far distant, unknown land.

"Guess I'd better set a trap for that coyote," he said. "Like as not he'll be after the chickens soon."

★ ★ ★ ★ ★

That was the life of America Jones. As his son I knew parts of the story; the rest I learned from the lips of my mother before she passed away. I have in my pocket the written offer of Frank Davis for the old place that I received some weeks ago at my home in the city.

Now I am waiting the arrival of my sister Murelda before I give Davis an answer. But I already know what the reply to the rancher will be, and I know that Murelda will side with me. A legacy provided by so great a love and at such personal, heartbreaking cost deserves better at the hands of its heirs than being auctioned off to the highest bidder.

THE RED EAGLE

CHAPTER ONE

"THE TRADING POST"

Beginning far up on the towering slopes of the Colorado Rockies the Río Grande flows like a twisting, silver ribbon through the deep cañons and along the gray-green hills of New Mexico—a place at times the turbulent and violent domain of certain Indian people—as it continues its way southward to Mexico.

Long before the white man touched the shores of the New World, the land and villages along its banks were ancient and furnished cool drink and welcome shade for the fierce warriors who roamed the sun-swept prairies that lie to the east and west and offer groves of cottonwood trees and stands of willow and cane for those who sought to hide when trapped in the bottom country.

Not too far removed from those dark-eyed braves was the boy who sat, that spring morning in the year of 1846, in front of a trading post lying near the Camino Real, or Royal Road, that follows along the river for a great deal of its length. He was of stocky build with thick, strong shoulders and muscular arms, and his eyes, dark and set well apart in a broad, mahogany-toned face, were calm and level as he watched the stagecoach pull up and come to a stop before the building.

The trading post of Amos Underwood was not a regular stop for the coach, but the driver had long been friends with the tall, wind- and sun-tanned trader and his wife, and he always paused there to give his horses and his passengers a brief rest before starting out on the last lap of the trip for the town of El Paso. Three people got off the stage, along with the driver, and walked into the shadowy coolness inside the low structure with its eighteen-inch-thick adobe walls, and the boy watched them in his quiet, thoughtful way. One of the passengers, apparently a trapper since he was dressed in fringed buckskins, paused as he was entering the door and spoke.

"Hy, there, younker," he said with a smile. "You waiting for the stage to take you somewhere?"

The driver answered him. "Nope, that's Donald Red Eagle. Lives here with the Underwoods. They picked him up at a massacre once."

"Sure tell he's an Apache," the trapper commented, and moved on.

Donald Red Eagle heard and understood what the two men had said for during the years he had been with the Underwoods he had learned a fair amount of the English language, and, while he much preferred to speak in Spanish or in the tongue of the Apache people, he tried to show his appreciation to the trader and his wife for the many things they had done for him by doing as they wished and using their words. Spanish, however, was the language most often used along the frontier, and it was only when he was alone with old Cocospero that he had the chance to speak in Apache.

He half turned then, listening for sounds of the former chieftain of the western Mescalero tribe, but he heard nothing, and he swung slowly back, letting his eyes again drift out over the mesa and low hills beyond the river to the east. The mountains were no more than a ragged, grayish blur, so far distant were they, and many times he had wondered what lay within their rough, forbidding outlines. No one he talked to had known, not even Cocospero who had journeyed to many distant places when he was young and strong, but someday Donald Red Eagle would go; he would learn for himself; he would see what was in the gray hills and even what was on the far side, and perhaps he would learn something of his father.

He sighed. To go there would be a long time away. One had to cross the terrible Jornado del Muerto, the Journey of the Dead, a vast, treeless, and waterless land of desert that all men feared and avoided and that had been the finish for many unwary travelers—no place for a boy of a scant twelve summers. But, someday, go there he would, someday when he had a fine horse and a pack mule and a rifle and such things as the white men had.

"Donald!" Mrs. Underwood called from the doorway, and he slid off the pile of wood and faced her. She was a large woman with almost snow-white hair. Her eyes were kind, and, when she smiled, it made him want to smile, too. "Are you dreaming again?"

He nodded, looking down at his heavy shoes. Someday, when he was older, he would change those; someday he would wear Apache moccasins and leggings like Cocospero and not those stiff, awkward leather boxes that made quiet trailing through the forests impossible. Usually, if it was a hot trail, he removed the shoes, but he was always careful to put them back on before he returned to the post.

"About your father?" Mrs. Underwood said kindly. "Were you thinking about him again?"

Donald Red Eagle nodded once more. "Someday I will find him," he murmured.

"I know you will," Mrs. Underwood replied. "When you have grown up to be a big, fine man, then you will start to search for him. But do not plan too much on finding him, Donald. Mister Underwood has told me several times that he does not think he is alive."

"But there was a man who escaped the massacre."

"Yes, I know. A few, but it means that, if one of those had been your father, we would have heard from him by now . . . after six years."

"Maybe he doesn't want me," Donald Red Eagle said in a low voice.

Mrs. Underwood stepped from the doorway and laid her hand upon the boy's shoulders. "You must never say that again, Donald. Your father would want you, if he were alive. I'm afraid that's the reason, though. I'm sure he isn't alive."

"I've got to know for sure," the young Apache said. "I have to find out for myself."

"You will when you get older," Mrs. Underwood said, and moved aside as the passengers came back out to the stage. Amos Underwood followed them, talking with the driver, and Donald heard him say as the man climbed up into his seat on top of the coach: "Well, if there's Indian trouble coming, we ought to get word to the soldiers at the fort."

"I'll pass it along," the driver said, and kicked off the brake. His long whip snaked out over the four horses and cracked, and the team lunged forward. The coach jerked into motion, rocking back and forth on its springs, and swung out onto the road in a swirl of dust, the yelling of the driver floating back to them in the hot air. The trader stood for a long minute, watching the Concord disappear, a disturbed look on his face.

"What is it, Amos?" his wife asked in an anxious tone.

"Looks like we may be in for trouble," he said, turning about. "Some of the Indians have gone on the warpath and have been attacking the travelers and settlers south of here.

And to the west, so the driver said."

"But, we've never been bothered by them. They never come around here."

"I know," the trader replied. "They never have . . . but there's always a first time." He spun about on one heel and faced Donald. "You and Cocospero had better take the wagon and haul in a good supply of wood and feed," he said. "No telling what might happen. We might have to hide up here for several days, and we want to be ready if anything does happen."

Donald Red Eagle nodded, and turned for the corral in the back of the trading post. The place was arranged something like a fort, the main buildings being in the front with a high fence of rock and cedar posts running out behind it and enclosing a large area in which stock and supplies were kept. He was thinking deeply as he opened the gate and entered the yard: there must be real danger of an attack, for he had seen it there on Mr. Underwood's face, and the thought came to him that the trader had not told all he knew, apparently not wanting to worry his wife. He wished he knew which tribe was causing the trouble, and he wondered if it might be his people. But how would he know? The Apaches were split into many tribes, and the tribes had even split into smaller units from time to time. He knew he was of the Mescalero branch, that he was not a Chiricahua or of the Western clans, but that didn't help very much. The Mescalero people ranged from the mountain country around the town called Santa Fé, deep into the land of the Mexican people, from the hills in the west to an unknown distance eastward. Thousand upon thousand of square miles.

He turned then toward the hut where Cocospero lived. Perhaps the old chief could tell him more of it.

CHAPTER TWO

"A FALLEN CHIEF"

Donald Red Eagle entered the low doorway of the hut and paused, letting his eyes become accustomed to the gloomy darkness of the small room. He heard a movement to his left, and then Cocospero, speaking in Apache, said: "Come in, little son."

The boy stepped inside, closing the door to block out the rising heat of the day, and dropped to his haunches against a wall. The slowly resolving figure of Cocospero began to take form in the opposite shadows as his eyes adjusted themselves, and he remained silent as he knew the old chief expected him to. Talking was never a thing to be hurried. Talking was something that must be done deliberately and slowly and with a great deal of thought.

He saw then that Cocospero was mending a moccasin, sewing on a small leather patch with a bone needle and a strip of sinew, and that he was standing so that the single faint ray of light working in from the room's one small and round porthole window might enable him to see. This was woman's work, this sewing business, and the pride of the old brave would not permit his going outside where he might see better to work. He was typical Apache, this Cocospero, squat, wide-shouldered, and wide-faced. He had small, black eyes that were sharp as arrow points, and, although he had suffered a wound in one leg that left it stiff, he could move quickly for his seventy years, and the strength in his arms had always amazed Donald.

"You come from the good white-eyes?" he said in Apache tongue.

51

The wisdom of the old chief was another source of wonder to the boy. He seemed to know everything beforehand; he always knew what another was thinking, and he could reach far back into his memory and bring up things that gave the answer to some problem of that present day. And when they were together in the forests and the groves along the river, he was a never-ending fund of information about the birds and the animals that moved about. Nothing escaped his glance, and he was a calm and patient teacher, imparting his knowledge to little Red Eagle.

The boy said: "I do, Grandfather."

Cocospero worked patiently at his mending. "He has need of me?"

"Of us both," Donald said. "He fears an attack by unfriendly Indians and wishes us to haul in wood and feed."

Cocospero stopped then, and his eyes lifted up to the high window and looked out into the sky. "It is begun," he said in a soft voice.

Red Eagle waited a time and then asked: "What is begun, Grandfather?"

The old chief was actually no relation to him, but in speaking the boy used the general form of politeness customary among the tribes. Had he been of similar age he would have addressed him as "Brother."

"The last of peace," Cocospero murmured, and turned his gaze to the boy. He laid the moccasin aside and came noiselessly across the room, sitting down beside Red Eagle. "The time that I feared has come. The time when there will be no peace in the valleys or on the mesas or in the hills. Everywhere will there be great trouble, and no man shall walk in safety."

Donald Red Eagle shifted on his heels, disturbed by such words. "You knew this would someday happen?"

"I knew, I knew," Cocospero said, "and for that I am here

52

now, small warrior. Like my own son I have taught you the ways of the Apaches that, living here among the white-eyes, you must not forget. Now as a father might tell his own son the story of his life, I tell you that which is in my own heart."

Cocospero paused, his eyes resting upon his gnarled, brown hands. For a time he rubbed his fingertips together, and then, in a distant, faraway voice, he began: "Once I was a great medicine chief of the Mescaleros. Our tribe was strong, and we lived in the tall grass country near the river that flows to the sunset without end, the Gila. We had a great herd of good horses, and we were rich in plunder for our men were brave and daring, and they halted many of the *nakai-yes* wagon trains coming from the south.

"Our war chief was a great man, as brave as Unsen ever let upon this earth, but he was also a proud man, and he did not always heed my advice and the warnings I read in the flames of the fire or heard in the call of the evil one, the owl bird. And many times he accused me of having the heart of a chicken and the spirit of a coyote, but these things I did not mind. We were a great and strong people, and of those things I was proud. We were respected by all other Apaches and feared by the Pueblo people who live in villages and grow corn and raise sheep and cattle to the north and west of us, and the *nakai-yes* sent many soldiers to slay us and capture us, but we made foolish ones of them all."

Cocospero stopped. He arose and moved to the door in his halting step, and for a moment he let his gaze drift about the post yard and to the low hills beyond the fence and their now dazzling heat glaze. "But one thing I knew. It was a battle we would never win completely. We could turn back the *nakai-yes* . . . we could rob their *conductas* of wagons, but they always came again. They left, but they returned. And then one day we saw a white-eyes, a *mer-hi-kano* in our land. Soon more came and more after that. They were friendly people but stern, and they laughed when the war chiefs threatened them, and by that I knew they would never be frightened.

"They came looking for the *pesh-klitso,* the yellow iron called gold, and our mountains rang with the sounds of their hammers and picks. There was trouble. Some were killed, and some of our people were killed, also, for the white-eyes carried the *pesh-e-gah,* the stick that shoots death, and we had only arrows and lances at first. But it made little difference. The white-eyes fought and laughed and died . . . and more came, and I knew that our day of glory was coming to sunset. Soon it would end.

"A meeting was called of all the Mescaleros. It was held in the big cañon of the long rocks, and all the war chiefs and the medicine chiefs and the bravest warriors sat around the big fire and talked of the white-eyes. Many wanted to take to the path of war and kill them all, but such was useless. They came from the north in a stream as steady as the water in the river. Others desired to be their friends and would let them go in peace, but there was much talk against our giving up our lands to them.

"It came my time to speak, and I said what was in my heart, and what I had foreseen in the power of my *hod-den-tin* medicine. There should be peace with the white-eyes. We could not drive them out, for, as we grew fewer, they became stronger, and no man who laughs when he fights and faces death is a coward and can be defeated. Once we took to the ways of war, we would become lost forever. It was written."

Cocospero turned and came back to the boy, sitting down once more beside him. "At once the great war chiefs arose and talked against me, saying I was afraid, that I was traitor to the Apache people. But I was not. I was telling truth as I saw it in the days to come, but they would hear me not. The meeting ended, and the tribes went back to their lands, and I became as one alone. My tribe no longer would permit me to dwell in their circle of wickiups, for I was dishonored and no longer one of them.

"A summer passed, and I came here to live and work for the good white-eyes Undah-wood, for it is not good to live alone in the valleys and in the mesas, and I have learned much. The white-eyes would be our friends and not our enemy, but either way they will come, and they are as numberless as the trees upon the mountains. And now, if the tribes have voted to make war upon them, the days of the Apache people will soon end, for they cannot stop the coming of the white-eyes."

Donald Red Eagle said: "Was it not the evil white-eyes that brought about the massacre of my father's tribe? Is it not said truly that all white-eyes will kill their brothers for the yellow iron?"

Cocospero placed his sharp gaze upon the boy. "Do you believe the white-eyes Undah-wood would do so?"

Donald shook his head. "But he is good. Others are not like him."

"Little warrior, because one man is bad, do not think all men of his tribe are bad, also. All Apaches are not good. There are also bad ones, just as there are many good white-eyes who love the Indian as a brother and would help him and never do him harm."

"Do you think it could be my people who are taking to the path of war against the *mer-hi-kanos?*"

Cocospero considered the question for a long time. "It is Apaches, for the Pueblos are a beaten people, and the Comanches come not that far from their homes. Likely it is the Mescaleros and the Chiricahuas, but of which band I would not know. I think it is not your people, my son."

"Why? My people have cause for vengeance against the white-eyes."

"Listen well, Red Eagle, and I will tell you again of the massacre. Then ask your own mind if there could be any who would take up the lance and the arrow."

CHAPTER THREE

"MASSACRE IN THE MOUNTAINS"

"Juan José," Cocospero began, "was a great chief of the Apaches. He was known far and wide as a man who spoke with a straight tongue, and he was respected by all, even by the *nakai-yes* who sent many soldiers to fight against him but were never able to capture him. His tribe was strong and rich, and they did well along the Camino Real and the other trails, and it was said that the braves of his band had never been beaten in battle.

"Like all Apaches they moved around from time to time, but they liked best of all the mountain country where the grama grass was tall and the water from the streams cold and clear. They lived mostly near the *cobre* country to the far west of here, and many of the other tribes envied them their wealth.

"But there was greater danger to come. Danger from the *nakai-yes* who had grown tired of the ceaseless raiding of wagon trains and who prevailed upon their government to send more soldiers into our land. This did no good. Juan José was smart and his warriors brave, and the soldiers returned to Mexico much fewer in numbers and much wiser in the ways of war. But the merchants did not give up, and they prevailed again upon their government, and this time they offered a plan of their own. They would pay to any man the sum of two hundred and fifty dollars in the white iron called *sil-vah-peso* for each Apache warrior killed and smaller amounts for the woman captured.

"There was a white-eyes in our land then called by the name of John-sohn and another called Glee-sohn. They were our friends, and they came and went as they pleased among our people without harm, but they knew well and best Juan José, and they spent much time in his camp in the mountains. One time they went upon a journey, and for many sleeps they did not return, and, when they did, they had with them many white-eyes, one of them being the good Undah-wood.

"These strange white-eyes were buying mules, and John-sohn and Glee-sohn, knowing that Juan José had many and was their friend, took them to his camp that they might bargain. They had come from the land of the *nakai-yes,* and it was rumored that John-sohn was now their friend, but this he denied when Juan José asked him.

" 'I am your friend,' he said, and because he had spoken before to Juan José, and the chief knew he did not speak with a forked tongue, he did believe him.

"So a great feast was held by the tribe. Fires were built, and venison and mule meat was barbecued, and great pots of stew were prepared. The men sat around and talked and smoked and told of many things while the women kept the food ready, for this was a meeting of friends, and there was no hurry to get to the business of mule buying and trading. The other white-eyes were vastly impressed by the ways of the Apache people, and they watched and admired the strength of the Mescalero men when they performed in contests.

"The feasting and the games lasted well through the night,

and Holos was rising from behind the mountains in the east when the last sound had gone and all had fallen asleep."

Cocospero paused, listening. Outside somewhere a meadowlark was pealing his musical whistle, filling the still, hot air with its lilt. Pans rattled in the kitchen of the main building, and Donald Red Eagle recalled the chore that was yet to be done. But he said nothing. He had heard the story of the mountain massacre many times from the old chief's lips, but it never tired him. He waited for him to go on.

"Near noon time the men began to awaken, and Juan José told the white-eyes to bring up their stock. He was ready to bargain with them. The strange men did, driving their burros and pack horses into the yard in front of the wickiups and there began to unload their sacks of cloth and beads and such trinkets as our people like.

"When it was all spread upon the ground, Juan José said . . . 'There are no rifles, no guns for trading. Why do you not bring such things as those to trade with us?' "

"The white-eyes Undah-wood said . . . 'Never will I be guilty of giving the Indian people guns for they mean only great trouble. Nor will I ever bring them whisky, the fiery water that turns all men's minds and makes them bad.'

" 'It is guns and bullets for them we want,' Juan José answered, but the white-eyes shook his head.

" 'We can do no business, then,' he said, and began to pick up his trading stock.

"The man John-sohn called out then, saying . . . 'Come to my pack, good friends. I have many presents for you here.' And Juan José and his braves and the women and children hurried over to where he stood near his mule. His pack was open on the ground. And there were a great many things of beauty for them all to choose from.

"They gathered around the pack and began digging in the

pile of gifts when suddenly the man Glee-sohn, who was standing near his own pack mule, drew a strange kind of *pesh-e-gah* from a saddle blanket where it was hidden and exploded it straight into the crowd. It was a new kind of gun, it having a large tube from which came all manner of bullets in small pieces of iron, and many people fell when it struck.

"Then a great cry went up at this deceit, and the other white-eyes rushed in to stop John-sohn and Glee-sohn, but they could not, for John-sohn turned his gun upon them and threatened to shoot, while Glee-sohn exploded his strange *pesh-e-gah* again, and more of our people fell to the ground. Many were killed and many lay dying, and those who tried to crawl away into the brush were shot by the two false friends, and it was realized that they were working for the *nakai-yes* and had spoken without truth to Juan José when he had questioned them. When none of the band was left standing, John-sohn and Glee-sohn began to move among them, taking back the things that were given to them as gifts and such things that were not theirs but they desired.

"The other white-eyes would have helped the injured, but John-sohn and Glee-sohn would not let them and told them to go on their way as they had no need of them now, it being just a trick they used when they brought them to Juan José's camp to get all the people together. They pointed their guns at the men, and they left, but as the white-eyes passed between the wickiups, the good Undah-wood saw a small boy hiding there, and he picked him up and took him with him that the evil John-sohn and Glee-sohn might not also kill him."

That boy had been Red Eagle, and Amos Underwood, shocked and horrified by what had taken place, brought the trembling youngster to his wife, and they raised him as their own.

"Never again did the man John-sohn or Glee-sohn look upon the Apache people, for their arrows were pointed at them, and it is not known if they escaped to Mexico or not, but it was said they were starved out and died in a trap the Chiricahuas threw about them when they heard of the massacre."

"Only I did escape," Red Eagle said.

"My sister who was sent to be a wife to one of Juan José's sub-chiefs lived for a short while. It was her thought that none escaped. When she was told of you, she said there were no others with such good fortune."

The boy stirred. "But did not the good white-eyes Undah-wood say some of the wounded might have crawled off into the brush and escaped to other tribes?"

"In truth, he said such was possible, but also he had great doubts. Many were killed trying to do so."

"But could not they have waited until John-sohn and Glee-sohn were gone? Could not they have played the waiting game, lying still as the yellow armadillo, pretending death and moving only when those men were gone?"

Cocospero laid his hand upon the boy's shoulder. "I fear you hope in vain, little warrior. Is it not enough to know your father was a brave and strong man?"

Donald Red Eagle shook his head. "It is not enough. I would know for sure, Grandfather. I would know many things . . . if my father is yet alive, if the two men John-sohn and Glee-sohn are yet alive, if I have any people still in this land. All these things I would know, and someday I shall."

"*Ai*, someday you shall," Cocospero agreed. "You are one who thinks much, Red Eagle, and there is in you the makings of a strong and wise chief."

"I would become a chief?"

"I see much help for our people should one day you become their chief, little warrior. Your heart is filled with the right thoughts. You have brave blood in your veins."

"How can I become a chief, living here with the white-eyes?" the boy said in a tired voice. "I know not where my people are, if there be any, or if they would have me among them should I return."

"You shall return someday. If not to your own band of the Mescaleros, to another, and they will welcome you as their brother. But this thing I tell you now . . . you shall use your wisdom for the good of all our people! You shall put behind you all thoughts of personal gain for yourself, and you shall think and do only for the tribe."

"But how will I know what is good and what is bad for all?" Red Eagle said, aroused at what the old chief was saying. After all, was such possible? Chieftainship among the Apaches is not passed down from father to son but is obtained by ability alone, and a man only becomes a tribal leader by his own efforts.

"Your heart will tell you, little warrior," Cocospero said. "When you have a great decision to make, listen to what it will say to you. That will be right."

"If I be chief someday, I will remember," the boy said.

Cocospero got slowly to his feet and moved to the doorway. "It is thus written, a great chief will arise after much trouble, and he shall unite the tribes in peace with all men. Now, shall we not do this thing the good white-eyes wishes us to do?"

Donald Red Eagle came up and followed the old chief through the door out into the full sunlight.

CHAPTER FOUR

"SHADOWS IN THE FOREST"

The many words of Cocospero burned slowly in Donald Red Eagle's mind as they drove along the sandy road that led to the thick grove. Thoughts of the massacre of John-sohn and Glee-sohn and their treachery, of the faint possibility that some of the people of Juan José had escaped and joined up with other bands of Mescaleros—and that his father, by the remotest hope, might be one of them. That such could be true was far from the mind of Cocospero, but until Red Eagle knew for sure, there would be no peace in his own mind.

He could remember little of the massacre. There were always feasts and celebrations of sorts and that one had been very like the others, and he probably had been playing with the other small children when it had taken place and somehow, by a stroke of good fortune, had been a little apart from them when Glee-sohn had fired into the crowd. He did remember the roar of the shots and the screaming, and inborn instincts had sent him scurrying behind the wickiups where Underwood had discovered him and lifted him up into the saddle with him. He remembered the long ride through the mountains and coming finally to Underwood's cabin. Underwood at that time was not operating the trading post. Red Eagle recalled being turned over Mrs. Underwood who made a great fuss over him. That probably was hardest of all to understand. Whereas he had once been left to grow up in the close-to-nature manner of the Apaches who feel that this teaches much in self-reliance to small boy children, he found he was now being carefully cared for, fed, and given a soft bed that made him ache at first with its comfort.

Clothing, too, gave him trouble, and it was months before the Underwoods were able to keep shoes upon his feet and a shirt upon his back, but they were patient people, and finally they wore him into the habit. He was a lost, frightened, little animal those first few months, but when Cocospero came and consented to stay, he began to lose some of his fear, and, as the years moved slowly by, he warmed gradually to the ways of the white man, although there remained always in the back of his mind the memory of those things that came naturally to him. The wagon trundled over the loose sand, and the sun's sharp rays drilled down upon them. But it felt good. The sun was the friend of all Apaches and the chief of their gods with the exception of Unsen, who was the greatest of all. It was Unsen who controlled the sky and the earth and the moon and the sun and all the stars, and it was Unsen who had put the first Apache upon the earth and given him good land and grass and water for his horses and supplied him with all the things necessary. But next to him stood Holos, the sun, the friendly god, and it was to him the Apache people turned their eyes each morning and night and thanked him for his presence.

They reached the edge of the grove, no words passing between them that entire distance of a mile or so that separated the trees and the trading post, and Cocospero turned the team northward, following a faint trail he had taken before that led eventually to a place where a great number of cottonwoods had been blown down during a storm long back and that now were excellent for firewood. The horses pulled gently along in the cool shade, their harness jingling as they walked and the wagon making its dry squealing noises where grease was needed.

A bird sped by overhead, and Cocospero turned quickly to the boy who said—"Dove bird."—and the old chief smiled. It was a game between them, when they were in this forest, and a bird flew by. It was Red Eagle's task to name it, and it would be remembered how many times he was wrong, which, during the past year, had been only a few times.

"A coyote traveled there," he said a little while later, pointing to a paw print in a moist area along the road.

"Could it not be a dog? The coyote is his half-brother, and their sign is very much alike."

"No, Grandfather, this is a coyote. See closely, he walks with his nails pulled inside. The dog is not so careful and makes small lines with his."

"You learn well, little warrior," Cocospero murmured, and pulled the team to a sudden halt. He sat perfectly still in the seat, his sharp eyes gazing into the leafy branches of a tree that overhung the rest, his face making no sign of what his thoughts might be.

Donald Red Eagle followed his gaze, making no sound, as he had been taught to do under such conditions, and, even as his eyes caught sight of the huge horned owl, it hooted and glided silently away to a new resting place.

"It is the owl bird," Cocospero said in a hollow voice. "Evil is near. Soon there will be trouble. It is a sign."

"What kind of trouble, Grandfather?"

"There is no way to know, little warrior. But be on guard. Be always ready. It will come soon."

He clacked the team into movement again, and a few minutes later they pulled into the clearing where the fallen cottonwoods laid and drew up beside the largest. They climbed from the seat, taking up their axes, when a low hiss from Cocospero froze Red Eagle once more. He stood motionless, awaiting some word from the old chief, and then he heard, also, the quiet *tunk-tunk-tunk* of a horse walking on the soft floor of the forest.

The sound was coming from the other side of the clearing, and from the corner of his eye Red Eagle saw Cocospero glance quickly to see if their team was hidden, which it was. Red Eagle dropped then to the ground, following the motions of the old chief, and they remained there, crouched and absolutely still as the sounds drew closer. After a moment the sounds stopped, and it seemed to Red Eagle as if the whole forest had quit breathing and waited in a tight, suspended hush to see who or what it was. No birds sang, the katydids that looked like tree leaves stopped their clacking, and even the team, as if realizing, was quiet and did not rattle the harness.

"Apache." Cocospero barely uttered the word.

Straining his eyes, Red Eagle saw the man. He stood just outside the clearing in the thick brush, only his head and shoulders visible. He had coal-black hair that hung to his shoulders and was cropped above his eyes, and his face was painted in thin bars of red and black that began on either side of his nose and ran back across his high cheek bones. The man's gaze roved about the clearing like a sharp knife, searching out everything, studying each fallen log, each clump of brush, each suspicious object. Red Eagle held his glance for a long, breathless moment. He feared he had been seen, and his heart jumped up into his throat, but the Apache's eyes slid on past him. For a long minute more the man continued his search, and then quite suddenly the man was gone. One instant he was there, the next he was not, but they did not move until once again they heard the soft walking of the horse and waited until it had died out.

Donald Red Eagle would have risen then, but Cocospero laid a hand upon his knee. "Do not make haste," he murmured, and they remained as they had been, and not until the birds began to sing once more in the trees around the clearing did the old brave give the sign that they should rise.

It was the first time Red Eagle had seen an Apache warrior, and the clear, sharp fierceness of the man thrilled him deeply. He turned to Cocospero.

"Why could we not call to him, Grandfather? We are Apaches, too. Would he not know us as friends?"

"Not as friends," the old man said in a sad voice. "We work and live with the white-eyes, and that makes us their enemy. To them we are the same as the white-eyes."

A frown crossed Red Eagle's brow. "If that be so, how then will I return to the tribe someday?"

Cocospero shook his head. "Have no fear of that. A way shall be provided, if such is to be."

"But if it is so, and they do not wish me to return and join . . . ?" The words died there as the boy realized what the consequences might be should he be unwelcome.

Cocospero said: "A brave man thinks little of death, small son. And you are brave."

Donald Red Eagle thought of that for a moment and then asked: "Why was the Apache here?"

Cocospero turned to his axe. "It was as the owl bird foretold. Trouble is near. He was a scout."

Donald Red Eagle picked up his own blade and moved to help the old chief, a curious feeling running through him. It wasn't fair, but it was something that sharpened his wits and made him alert, and like Cocospero he stopped many times in his work that afternoon to listen and search along the clearing with sharp eyes.

CHAPTER FIVE

"REPORT FROM THE SOUTH"

They completed loading the wagon with wood and started back up the long road to the trading post. They had seen and heard no more of the scout, and it was Cocospero's thought that he was alone and had been looking over the country and getting the lay of the land, possibly for future activity. Donald Red Eagle quickly saw that the old chief was greatly disturbed about it.

"You will tell the good white-eyes Undah-wood about the scout?"

Cocospero nodded his head. "It is always best to be well-prepared."

"You think there is danger to be faced by him . . . by us?"

"It is as the owl bird foretold."

They drove the wagon into the yard behind the buildings, and, while Red Eagle began to unload, Cocospero went inside to talk with Amos Underwood. He returned a few minutes later, his dark face stolid, and said nothing, and the boy asked no questions, it not being proper to do so. It took a full hour to unload and stack the lengths of cottonwood, and, since the day was yet young, they were turning the wagon about and starting for another supply when the distant, rapid sounds of a running horse coming up from the south stopped them. The rider apparently was in a great hurry and together Cocospero and Donald Red Eagle slipped from the wagon's seat and moved around to the front of the trading post.

They saw the horseman, a half-doubled figure bent low over the saddle, flying up the road. The noise of the pounding

67

hoof beats brought Amos Underwood and his wife into the doorway where they waited as the rider rushed into the yard and half fell from the lathered pony's back.

"The Indians!" he gasped. "They got the stage!"

Cocospero moved silently forward and took the man by an arm to assist him. The man turned to him, his eyes widening in surprise as he beheld the Apache, and he looked for a moment like he was going to reach for the pistol in his belt, but Amos Underwood stepped from the doorway, saying—"It's all right."—and took his other arm, and they helped him inside.

Red Eagle led the fagged horse into the back and stabled him, slipping quietly back inside to where the man sat in a chair, holding a cup of steaming coffee and breathing heavily. He apparently was a miner, being dressed in the clothing of such, and the fright of whatever experience he had just passed through lay upon him, turning his eyes nervous and wide.

"It happened just below Piñon Gulch," he said. "There where the cañon spreads out into a fist."

He stopped and gulped another swallow of coffee, letting his gaze travel about the room as if yet unsure that he was safe. He saw Cocospero, motionless in the dark shadows inside the door, and a shudder passed through him.

"I was working up on the side of the mountain, a couple hundred yards away. I heard the stage go by, and I stopped to look. The driver saw me and waved, and I waved back, and just then I saw the Apaches ride out. They came from all sides, yelling and whooping it up. I heard one or two gunshots. They didn't seem to have many guns."

"Were there many Indians?" Amos Underwood asked in his gentle way.

"About twenty-five, maybe thirty. The people in the stage began to shoot back, but they weren't doing much good. The stage was rocking real bad as the driver whipped up the horses. He was standing up, and I saw an arrow hit him in the shoulder and just stick there. For a minute I thought he was going to fall, but he didn't. He just kept right on driving that team, trying to get away."

"Jess Conger was a good man," Underwood said in a low voice. "One of the best."

"He didn't have a ghost of a chance to get away," the miner said. "One of the horses fell, and the coach swerved around and turned over, and the Indians closed in. I could hear them yelling, and then I got to thinking about myself, and I got on my horse and headed for your place. I tried to keep out of sight, but they saw me. They started after me, but I had a little start, and my horse was fresh, and they didn't get within gunshot, but, by George, for a time there I wouldn't have given much for my chances."

"Did they follow you clear to my place?" the trader asked after a moment.

"Almost. They could see where I was headed for."

"Do you know if they turned back or did they just stop?"

The miner shook his head. "That I do not know."

The trader walked thoughtfully to the doorway, and for a long time he stood there, looking off toward the road, in the direction of Piñon Gulch from which the man had come. "It is possible that they are still there," he said in a low voice, "waiting for the others to come up." Suddenly he turned to Cocospero. Speaking in Spanish, he said: "What do you think, old one? Will they attack us now, or will they wait and come another time?"

"They will not come this day," the old chief said. "They will return to their camp with the spoils of their raid, and to-night they will have a feast and do much dancing."

"When will they come?" Underwood pressed.

"Tomorrow they will come."

The miner got slowly to his feet, a frown on his brow and his eyes hard with suspicion. "How does he know?" he asked in a harsh voice. "How does he know so much about it? You sure he's not one of them . . . a spy or something?"

Underwood said: "Don't worry about Cocospero. He's not one of them now. Once, perhaps, but not now. But he is an Apache, and he knows their ways."

"And the kid . . . how about him?"

Underwood stiffened, and his face went cold. "That boy has every reason to hate white men, friend, but you need have no fear of him, either. He has been a son to us for several years, here in our home."

"I don't know," the miner said with a shake of his head. "Indians don't change much. You can't trust them."

"There are white men who cannot be trusted, also," Amos Underwood commented and, motioning to Cocospero and Donald, moved out through the back door and into the yard. "We must be prepared," he said, when they were beyond hearing. "Find all the buckets and barrels and fill them with water. Set them in different places around the post. Be sure there are several upon the roof. We must expect fire arrows. Be sure the fence is strong and have the gate ready for quick closing."

"I shall close it now," Cocospero said, but the trader stopped him.

"Wait. There may be others who will come. It should be open to admit their teams. We can shut it quickly." He paused, mentally checking off the things that should be done, and then remembering: "Do not take another trip for wood. Do not leave the post any more until it is once again safe for us all." He dropped a hand upon Red Eagle's shoulder. "You will help Cocospero and do what he tells you, youngster."

The trader swung back toward the buildings, but halfway he hesitated and turned about, his glance touching Cocospero. "We are as brothers, old one?" he said in a questioning tone.

The old chief nodded. "It grieves me that my friend would think otherwise," he murmured, and turned away.

CHAPTER SIX

"ECHO OF TROUBLE"

Near the middle of the afternoon two more miners came in from the west, the news having been relayed to them by others seeking safety elsewhere, and close to sundown the eastbound stage that crossed the Camino Real some miles below thought better of the usual schedule and forsook its regular route, doubling back up to Underwood's place where it drove into the yard and unloaded its six passengers, five men and a girl. Red Eagle helped the driver stable the horses, and then, when full darkness fell, he went inside where all the others were gathered in the main room.

But this was not like other such times. There was no laughing and loud talking or singing or square dancing such as generally took place when several white people got together. Tonight they were quiet, and there was a grimness about the men as they smoked and now and then checked their handguns and long-barreled rifles.

Red Eagle could feel the tension in the room, and it grew steadily as night closed in, but Cocospero had told him there was little chance of there being a raid that night—in the early morning, perhaps, but not sooner. He could see that Amos Underwood was taking no chances, however.

"There will be a good moon tonight," the trader said, calling on everyone's attention. "We will take turns at sentry duty on the roof. Each man will stand a two-hour watch. I don't think we will be bothered, but we will leave nothing to guess. I will start now. You decide between you who will follow." He wheeled about to the ladder that stood just outside the door and, with his long rifle, climbed to the roof, Cocospero close behind him.

Donald Red Eagle sat quietly in the corner of the room, listening to the low drone of conversation. The female passenger of the stage said to the driver: "How long will we have to stay here?"

The driver shrugged. "Hard to say, ma'am. Maybe a day, maybe a week."

"Maybe forever," one of the miners observed, and the driver looked at him sharply.

"But I'm supposed to meet my family . . . in Kansas City," the girl said in a protesting voice.

"I'm sorry, ma'am, but we can't take chances with the Apaches. It's dangerous to be traveling right now."

"Now, really," the girl said in a doubtful way, "are the Indians as bad as all that? Why, the newspapers at home say that the trouble is all over. The soldiers have quieted them down, and they won't harm anybody."

"Maybe somebody ought to go get that newspaper feller and let him find out first hand!" one of the miners said, and laughed.

"And the Army, too. Somebody ought to tell them they didn't finish their job!"

"Now, really," the girl said again, and stopped, seeing the look in the driver's eyes. "I'm sorry. I don't mean to doubt you, but I am in such a hurry to get home."

"We all are, miss," one of the male passengers said. "But in times like these it never pays to take chances, and I think Mister Cabot, our driver here, was wise to turn off and come to this place for protection. At least, we're safe here. Likely the soldiers will show up, and we can have an escort when we leave."

"No soldiers closer'n Santa Fé," the miner said.

"A long way off," observed another of the passengers, a well-dressed man wearing a derby hat.

Silence hung for a few minutes, and Red Eagle could hear the far-away trilling of a mockingbird, somewhere down in the grove along the river. The music was clear, drifting in on the still, hot air.

"Why don't they keep the soldiers down here where they are needed?" the girl asked, after a time.

"Big territory," Cabot said, "and they never have enough men to patrol it right. They go one place, trouble breaks out another. Take four or five times as many men as they have now to do a proper job."

"Well, haven't the Indians been pretty quiet around here?" somebody asked.

"Well, yes," Cabot replied. "Up until a few years ago we had more trouble with the Mexican government than with the Indians. They didn't like the idea of the Americans coming in here, at all, and they were always arresting somebody and carting them off to Mexico City for trial. Guess they didn't like the fact that the Indians and the Americans got along pretty well, either, because they never had been able to make any sort of peace with the Apaches."

"What happened then?" the derby-hatted man asked.

"There was an old chief named Juan José," the stagecoach driver began, and Red Eagle came to sharp attention upon hearing the familiar name. He leaned forward on his bench, and it seemed to him that no one in the room breathed, it was that still. "He was the leader of a band of Mescaleros south of here a ways, and he was always a good friend of the Americans. One fellow named Johnson was particularly friendly with him, but this man Johnson fell in with the Mexican merchants on a deal where he was to be paid a good price in silver for every Apache he could kill and prove by bringing in their scalps. He went into partnership with a fellow named Gleason, and they got Juan José to get all his people together one day on some trumped-up cause and then massacred the whole band with a blunderbuss loaded with scrap iron."

"He killed all of them?" the girl said in a horror-filled voice.

"So far as I know. Never heard of any of them getting away."

Red Eagle felt Mrs. Underwood's eyes shift to him, but he did not look, and she said nothing. His own hopes sagged a little as he listened, for here again was word that none had escaped—but this man could be wrong, too. He was not aware that Red Eagle had been spared.

"Anyway," Cabot continued, "from that day on we began having trouble. Not all at once but in little bunches. A raid took place here and then some place else. There would be peace for a time, and then the report would come in about a settler being burned out or a miner found with a half dozen arrows in his back. We just never knew when or where it was going to crop up."

"But it was Johnson and Gleason that started it all. Why would they take it out on other Americans?"

"Apaches are funny people," the coach driver said. "There are several different tribes, but they don't particularly like one another . . . a sort of armed truce exists between them at all times. But when one band had trouble with the Americans, they all rose up and began to take their vengeance. It seems to be the one thing they agree upon, along with their hatred for the Mexicans."

"Perhaps," the man with the derby said slowly, "the Juan José affair was just something that set them off. I think they've been secretly opposed to the Americans coming down into their country for a long time, just as the plains Indians were. All they needed was a good reason to start things."

"Apaches never need a reason for anything," one of the miners said.

"That's true," Cabot said. "You never know why they do a thing or when they might."

"One thing is certain," the man in the derby hat said, "they're wasting their time trying to keep the Americans out of here. They'll flock down through here regardless of anything, and the Apache people would be smart to realize that. Sure, there will be a lot of Americans killed. But that won't stop them. It never has."

Red Eagle listened, hearing in those words the faint echoes of the meanings in Cocospero's warnings and admonitions earlier. It was as he had said: the Apache people would wage a losing battle against such a thing.

"Whatever happened to Johnson and Gleason?" one of the miners asked.

Cabot said: "Johnson got his. The Indians trapped him and fixed him good. Gleason got away."

Gleason got away! A small light began to burn inside Red Eagle when he heard these words. Gleason escaped—the man who had murdered his people! The light grew stronger, and a voice, deep in his brain, marked down those words, and he made a silent vow to himself. One day he would find Gleason, the Glee-sohn Cocospero spoke of, and he would settle with him. One day he would find him.

CHAPTER SEVEN

"THE RAID"

The Apaches struck at dawn.

A rattle of gunshots awakened Red Eagle, and he opened his eyes but remained perfectly still as old Cocospero had taught him to do under such circumstances, listening and waiting until he was sure.

"Little warrior," came the old chief's soft whisper into his ear.

The boy sat upright, and another crackle of guns broke across the half light of the early morning. Faintly he could hear shouting, coming from outside the post.

"You hear?" Cocospero asked.

"Yes, old Grandfather. It is the Apaches making their raid."

"It is as the owl bird foretold. Come quietly with me into the yard. We have much to do."

Red Eagle slipped swiftly into his clothing and hurried to the outside. In the gray dawn he could see the men stationed along the yard at various points, covering all sides, firing their guns at the Apaches who circled the trading post on their ponies. A few arrows were dropping into the yard, but none had found a mark. Up on the roof he could see the crouched figure of Amos Underwood and another man who fired and reloaded their rifles with steady regularity. Mrs. Underwood and the girl from the stagecoach moved in and out of the building, carrying powder and ammunition, their faces strained and drawn with worry.

"Watch you for fire arrows," Cocospero murmured to Red

Eagle. "You are young and move swiftly. The men must not leave their places at the wall."

Red Eagle moved hurriedly away and climbed to the roof where the trader and the other man were, and, when he turned to watch the yard, Red Eagle saw the old chief was starting out across the mesa toward the red flare of sunrise in the east. He began then a slow circle of the yard, alert for fire arrows and also for others that might strike him, but as the morning wore on, and none came, he stopped near his hut and rested in the scant shade.

The men were firing irregularly, and some of the shouting outside had fallen off. At noon Mrs. Underwood and the girl carried food to each of the men, and they ate where they stood, not daring to abandon their posts. No one talked much, and Red Eagle did not leave his place upon the roof. The sun beat down more intensely, and the sharp smell of gunpowder began to hang within the yard. The hours dragged by, and the tension began to tell. The stage driver, Cabot, began to swear in a steady stream from his corner, and one of the others suddenly jerked off his hat and sailed it out at the thin line of circling Apaches. Red Eagle watched it, wondering at the man's actions, but the Indians failed to notice it, and it struck the ground on its brim and rolled crazily about.

Four o'clock. Five o'clock. The sun dropped lower in the west. Cocospero left his hut and crossed the yard and mounted to the roof where Red Eagle waited and watched.

"It will be soon now, little warrior," he said. "When the sun ball drops behind the mountains, then will they try their best."

Almost at the moment Cocospero had predicted, the yelling increased, and the arrows began coming in thicker clouds. The men stepped up their firing, and Red Eagle,

77

risking a glance, saw the Apaches were tightening their circle, drawing in closer as they rode low upon their horses. He saw the first fire arrow then. He saw the Indian who shot it, and he watched as it soared like a falling star into the yard. But it fell harmlessly in the middle where there was nothing but hard ground, and he let it burn itself out.

As the circle of Apaches drew closer, the shooting of the men began to tell, and Red Eagle could see four or five riderless horses racing wildly about in the noise and confusion and one of the figures lying still upon the ground, the others being beyond the range of his vision. Strangely the fight seemed to affect him little, and he found himself doing the task assigned to him in a mechanical sort of way and feeling no particular fear for the relentless, closing circle beyond the fence.

The man with the derby hat spun suddenly about, and Red Eagle saw him jerk at the arrow sticking from his shoulder. Half the arrow came away in his hand, but the other half remained, and, swaying a little, he moved back to his place along the wall. A shower of fire arrows came over them, and at once the boy began dousing them with the water they had provided him. Before he could extinguish them all, another shower followed, some going onto the stable where they stuck upright, like torches. Mrs. Underwood came running from the trading post to help, and she fought them out, but again there came another dozen onto the roof, and Red Eagle grabbed up another bucket of water and came down from the roof to help her.

The man with the derby hat was sprawled out on the ground, and Mrs. Underwood, as soon as the fire arrows had been put out, took up his gun and powder and stepped into his place. Somewhere in the half gloom Cocospero moved tirelessly between the men, carrying supplies to them.

"Ammunition!" Amos Underwood shouted from the roof,

and Red Eagle saw the girl climbing the ladder with a new supply. Halfway up she hesitated and seemed to lose her footing, but after a moment she came on. More fire arrows descended, and now a flame was moving along the roof behind Underwood, and the girl and the other man up there were trying to beat it out, their pails of water evidently having been used up. Red Eagle seized the pail nearest him and ran across the yard and handed it up the ladder to the man.

"Good boy!" he heard the trader cry to him. When he was back in the yard and glanced up to see if the flames were out, he could see only the dim outlines of the girl and the man. Amos Underwood was lying down.

The shouting was nearer, and the arrows were falling in greater numbers. Spots of fire studded the yard, and a strong blaze leaped and danced along the outside wall of the stable where trash had been allowed to accumulate. Mrs. Underwood was no longer at the same place, and Red Eagle saw her nowhere in the yard. One of the miners was slumped against the wall, and the man with the derby hat still lay where he had fallen. Arrows were descending in a steady stream, and suddenly a long, thin lance of fire came over the fence and thudded into the rear of the post building. It caught at once, and flames shot up along the sun-dried wood framework of the porch. Red Eagle raced across the yard with a bucket of water and dashed it against the fire but caused no more than a long sizzle, and, before he could refill the bucket, the porch was a solid mass of vivid orange flames.

The guns from the roof had stopped, and somewhere back in the yard a man howled as an arrow struck him. The shouting of the Apaches was very close, and the entire place seemed to be ablaze. Faintly Red Eagle heard a voice calling him, and he turned and ran toward the sound. Mrs. Underwood lay upon the ground near the fence, and, as he bent over her, she said: "Donald! Ride! Find some place to hide where they cannot find you!" She said no more, and he turned to do her bidding as he had done during the many days of the past years.

An Apache came suddenly over the wall and dropped into the yard, a fierce, terrible creature, half naked, knife in one hand, a short lance in the other. Firelight dashed against his painted body and flickered weirdly, and Red Eagle crouched behind a barrel and watched in fascination. One of the miners came from the shadows, firing his gun, and the Indian went over backward in a dense cloud of smoke, shrieking into the night. But more were following him, and they began to come over the wall from all sides, and the remaining men backed into a far corner and poured a continuous stream of bullets at them. The Apaches moved in, heedless.

"Little warrior," Cocospero said at his shoulder, and he flinched, startled. "It is time. Come."

On hands and knees they worked toward the gate, and in the faint light there the boy saw the broken-off shaft of an arrow sticking from the old chief's side! He touched it with his fingers, but Cocospero shook his head.

"Remove your white-eyes clothing," he whispered, and the boy did as he was told, stripping down to nothing. "Here is breechcloth," he said in a slow, labored way. "Put it on and they will think you are as other Apaches. My knife I give to you."

Red Eagle started to speak, but Cocospero laid a finger across his lips. "I will open the gate. Go softly, young son. Be not seen. Keep your eyes to the pointed hill that lies to the south of the sunrise. There you will find Mescaleros."

"You are not coming?" Red Eagle said, feeling all at once alone.

"I travel far this night," Cocospero said, "but with none

other. Go your way and remember well my words, for I have spoken truth to you. Farewell, little chief."

"Farewell, old Grandfather," Red Eagle said, and slipped toward the gate.

It opened a small narrowness, and he crawled through.

CHAPTER EIGHT

"TRAIL BY NIGHT"

Behind Red Eagle came the sounds of shouting and the crash of gunfire as the white men fought on against desperate and hopeless odds. Before him horses wheeled and raced back and forth as Apaches, not aware that their kinsmen had breached the wall, continued to shoot arrows into the yard and ride in their tight circle. One saw the open gate and plunged for it. Red Eagle flattened out upon the ground, and the man stumbled over him and went on, thinking perhaps he was a wounded brother. Slowly Red Eagle crawled away from the opening, keeping to the fence, in the shadows that lay close to it where the dim twilight did not touch. More warriors saw the open gateway and hurried through. The popping of guns dwindled until only one sounded, and finally it stopped.

A great shout went up then, and Red Eagle knew they were all running toward the stock. Foot by foot he moved along the wall, resting when he saw movement or heard a noise that was not identifiable. Ahead lay the open mesa, several hundred yards of sand and small growth not large enough to conceal him, and across it he must make his way before he could reach the protective covering of the grove near the river. Reaching the end of the wall, he lay quietly, considering his next move. If all of the Apaches were inside, it would be fairly simple. But there were some who remained with the horses, and it was to them that he turned his attention.

He could not stay here, he knew. Sooner or later he would be discovered by a prowling warrior, searching for spoils, and he dared not show himself for no boy of such tender years would participate in a raid. Nor could he risk speaking since the dialect of his tribe would be different from theirs most likely, and it would be one chance in hundreds that he would find himself in friendly hands. He saw then a pony standing, head down, a little to one side of the main group, and a plan formed quickly in his mind; a desperate plan, to be sure, but he could see no other course.

He waited until there were no Apaches close by, and, then rising, he walked boldly to the pony and leaped upon its back, grasping the single rope hackamore as he did so. The pony's head came up in surprise, and it shied away in a half circle for a moment, but he jerked it around and let it walk slowly through the other horses. A man shouted something to him, but it was an unfamiliar word, and he waved his hand and went on, little sharp-pointed prickles running up and down his back as he tried to act unhurried and at ease.

The warrior's voice challenged him again, and this time he caught the question: "Where do you go with my brother's horse? You have made a mistake."

He realized with a sinking heart that, of all the horses standing around, he had chosen one familiar to one of the braves left on guard. But there was no helping it now. He had reached the seemingly endless distance through the gather of ponies, and the mesa lay open before him. Ahead was the dark shadowy depths of the grove.

"Have you no hearing?" the Apache called out again.

Red Eagle kicked the pony in the ribs, and it leaped away. Instantly a shout lifted behind him, and, as he crouched low over the racing mount's neck, he heard the sudden pound as the guard gave chase. The sand flowed beneath him, and the bulky blur of the grove moved closer. An arrow swished overhead, and he drummed at the pony's ribs with his heels. The yells of his pursuer seemed nearer. Another arrow sped by, grazing his arm, and he tried to duck lower on the straining pony. The grove loomed before him with all its concealing darkness, and he shouted at the horse for greater speed, but all at once it seemed to pause, seemed to hang in mid-air, and he knew it had been hit. Its head flew up and its legs collapsed, and he was sailing through the darkness. He struck feet first, and the shock of it sent pain surging up through his body, but he dared not stop.

Automatically he cut sideways, and he heard the Apache rushing close by. Keeping low, he ran on, moving from bush to bush, staying in the black shadows. He heard other shouts then and knew that the first warrior now had help. He did not wait to consider but pressed on at a steady trot, taking no pains to conceal his trail. That would come later. It was necessary now to place all the distance possible between himself and the Apaches.

For hours he traveled, guided by the stars, in the general direction Cocospero had told him to go. Somewhere around midnight he stopped, hearing no sounds behind him, and crawled into a huge cottonwood where he rested for a time. Afterward, he moved higher into the tree, being careful not to scrape or mar the tree's bark, and worked out to the end of a wide-reaching limb. From there he dropped to the ground, erasing the prints where he had struck with the trailing leaves of a branch, and moved on, taking great care. Anyone following his path would come to a halt at the cottonwood, and from that point on it would be no easy matter to locate his course.

He pressed on until near daylight, and, thinking then it would be easier to watch his back trail, he swam the river at a shallow point and worked deeper into the brush on that side. He felt hunger, and, making a snare from one of the tough vines as Cocospero had taught him to do, he caught a young rabbit and roasted it over a small fire after which he moved for some distance, in case the fine wisp of smoke had been seen, and made himself a bed in a deep thicket of dogwood.

He slept but lightly and for a short time. When he awakened, the sun was scarcely started on its long climb, and, taking what was left of the rabbit, he moved on down the river, keeping well within the groves, and, when darkness overtook him that day, the pointed peak Cocospero had set out for him as a landmark was not so distant. But he had learned something else. It lay not near the river's course but far to the east, and that meant there would be a wide, barren mesa to cross, a broad expanse in which there would be no game, no water, and little cover if pursuers were following. He began at once to prepare himself.

He snared two more rabbits and roasted them that next morning. There were plenty of fish in the river, but Apaches would not touch them, having a truce with them as they did with the bear. Cocospero's teachings again had their effect, and Red Eagle let them be. From a gourd he fashioned a canteen for water, making a sling of a vine. Around noon of that next day he reached a point along the river that appeared to be opposite the pointed hill, and he rested there in the coolness of the willows until sundown. The mesa was no place to travel while the sun ball was overhead; he would start in the darkness and hope there would be a place for hiding when sunrise came.

It was easy walking over the smooth-packed sand, and the night was cool and the stars shone brightly down upon the vast quiet of the land. The moon had weakened, and its glow turned all things to a silver cast, and Red Eagle, making his solitary way across this seemingly endless world, felt a happiness within himself. This was his life, the coolness, the solitude, the bright stars and moon, and the joy of returning to it moved through him and left a feeling of gladness. He sobered then, thinking perhaps he would not be returning to it, and old Cocospero's words came to him; he might not be welcome, and, finding himself in such a position, he might not escape to seek a friendlier band of Mescaleros.

He shrugged, dropping the thought. Such things would be faced when the proper time came. No need to think of them now. He stopped, hearing the far-away yipping of a coyote coming out over the mesa in lonely, high tones. He waited, listening for an answer, but none came, and he knew the sound was genuine and no signal between men.

Daylight found him halfway across the wide, flat land, and he took refuge from the sun and any searching eyes beneath a bramble of greasewood. He ate a half of one rabbit and drank a little of his precious water after which he catnapped through the daylight hours, hearing and seeing no one. When darkness set in again, he was up and resuming the march toward the high peak, now very close.

That night was much like the other, and sometime early in the morning he felt the slight rising of the ground under his feet and knew that he was nearing the edge of the mesa and starting to climb the low hills. Fixing the peak before him, he bore straight for it, but before he had gotten a mile into the rough country, he stopped short. A drift of wind coming down to him bore the unmistakable smell of smoke. A camp was close by, and he sought out a place beneath some oak brush to wait until daylight.

The moment was at hand.

CHAPTER NINE

"RETURN TO THE TRIBE"

He waited until the sun was well started, lying there beneath the oak and eating the last of the rabbit and drinking what was left of the water. He left the gourd there and then moved out into the open and started boldly in the direction from which the smell had come and from which now came the barking of dogs. A little nervous excitement moved through him, and his throat became dry, but he walked slowly and firmly, and there were no traces of his feelings showing on the outside.

Perhaps he covered a quarter of a mile or a trifle more, but he heard the sound just as he breasted an open space, the faintest scraping as a moccasin rubbed against rock. He did not pause, knowing that he was watched and being followed and that soon they would make known their presence. He crossed the cleared area and let his eyes follow the streams of smoke from the camp, winding up into the early morning sky, and the noise of the dogs grew louder. The tension built up inside him to a near bursting point, and he had an urge to run, to dash away through the rocks and hide from those silent, watching eyes that followed him, but he knew that would be a fatal thing to do, and he grasped his nerves more firmly and kept on, expecting each step to be challenged.

The sharp point of the mountains raised up ahead of him, gray-green in the morning light, and he thought briefly of Cocospero and the Underwoods and the others who had been at the trading post. Things had happened so swiftly, there had been little time to think of them at all, the Underwoods because they had treated him well after saving his life and Cocospero who had taught him much wisdom and the ways of the Apaches and been his good friend. And for the others, too, because it was too bad to die.

"Hold!"

The command crackled out ahead of him, and an Apache warrior glided out from behind a great bulge of rock. He was stocky and painted, and he held a half-drawn bow in his hands. Red Eagle stopped and waited, keeping his eyes straight upon the man.

"It is but a boy," the warrior said, letting his bow relax. Another Apache came in beside him, and Red Eagle heard the noise behind him of a third.

"How are you called?"

"Red Eagle," the boy said.

"You speak the tongue of the Apache people but not of our tribe. Why are you here?"

"I look for my own tribe."

"You are lost?"

"I have been lost," Red Eagle said.

"Who is chief of your people?"

Red Eagle waited a moment. "Juan José," he said, and saw the men look at him with strange faces. There had been no other answer he could give.

"Come, we will go," one of the braves said, and moved in beside him, and he knew he had won a small victory. They were taking him to their camp and their chief.

It was not a large camp as camps go; two dozen or so wickiups clustered on the flat beneath the pointed hill. One large fire burned in the wide clearing inside the circle, and numerous small cooking flames smoked and danced around blackened pots that filled the air with strong good odors. The dogs rushed out to greet them, but the braves drove them back, and they marched the length of the camp while pairs of curious eyes followed them. They came to a halt before a larger conical dwelling.

An Apache stepped out and faced them, and the boy felt the strong, hard gaze of his eyes immediately. He was taller than the average tribesman, and his face was clean and sharp, and there was an air of strength and power about him. His glance raked Red Eagle up and down and shifted to one of the braves.

"This boy is not of our band," he said in a deep voice. "Is he a slave prisoner?"

"He is strange to us," one of the warriors said. "We found him coming to this camp. He seeks his people."

The chief turned back to the boy, standing stiff and still before him. "Of what people are you, young one?"

"Of Juan José," Red Eagle said.

The Apache's eyes grew even sharper. "Juan José is dead these many summers and his people with him. So you speak with a forked tongue."

Red Eagle squared his shoulders. "I speak English words. I did not die when the white-eyes struck down Juan José and his tribe."

The chief softened a bit, seeing the straight young figure so brave before him. "I am Black Cloud, chief of the Gray Hill Mescaleros. How are you called, young son?"

The boy told him, and the chief asked: "Where have you been these many summers since Juan José fell dead at the hands of the white-eyes?"

"I have been lost," Red Eagle said, and stopped, hoping

that Black Cloud would ask no more, but the thought came to him then that it would be better to be honest and not hold back the truth. It was not in him to lie, and, if he did not tell he had lived with the Underwoods, he would be doing just that. "I was taken by good white-eyes and lived with them."

"Why came you now?"

"There was a raid, and they with others are now dead. I escaped."

Black Cloud stared at him. "Where was this raid?"

"Four suns to the north and west."

To the crowd that had gathered silently around them Black Cloud lifted his eyes and murmured: "This young one speaks and acts as a brave warrior." To Red Eagle he said: "You lost not the ways of your people when you dwelled with the white-eyes. How explain you this?"

"There, also, lived an old Apache chief, forgotten by his tribe. He taught me well."

"How was he called?"

"Cocospero," Red Eagle said, and waited, fearing what the next words might be.

But Black Cloud shook his head. "I knew him not. Young son, your people are all dead, and there are none for you to find. Where go you now?"

"Are there no others who escaped?"

"None. A few lived but for the rising of the next sun and then departed. Who among them do you seek?"

"My father."

"How was he called?"

Red Eagle shrugged. "I know not, Chief Black Cloud. I hoped to find those who would remember."

"There are none to remember," the Apache chief said, "and you have no people awaiting you. What think you to do?"

The boy looked down, hope going out of him. "I know

not," he said. "Am I prisoner here among you?"

Black Cloud smiled faintly. "So bold and fierce a young warrior! Black Cloud respects all things as these."

"I then may go on in peace?"

"If it be your will, but you have no people, Red Eagle, and we have need of brave men here. Stay with us and make my people your people, our camp your camp."

"It is a great honor the chief Black Cloud gives to me," Red Eagle said in a serious voice, and again the tall Apache smiled faintly.

"You have the size of a twelve-summer boy but the mind and tongue of a grandfather," he said. "Someday I think you will do great things."

"I will serve only my chief," the boy said.

"Then with us shall you remain," Black Cloud said. "You shall be of this tribe, and you shall become the son of Walking Pony, since you have no father, and live with him in his wickiup. He shall teach you our ways as he does teach our other young men, and, when the time comes, you shall take your place with the men. It is done."

"I am grateful, my chief," Red Eagle said, and turned away as a hand dropped lightly upon his shoulder.

CHAPTER TEN

"SON OF WALKING PONY"

The man he faced was old, almost as ancient as had been Cocospero. He was dressed as were the others, breechcloth, moccasins, a strip of red cloth around his head to hold his black hair in place and in which two eagle feathers had been thrust. His face was very wrinkled, but his eyes were clear and bright, and they sparkled a little when he spoke.

"I am Walking Pony, little son. Come."

He wheeled about, and Red Eagle followed him through the crowd across the camp to a small wickiup. An old squaw met them in the opening, and Walking Pony told her the boy was their son and would live with them, at which she grunted and moved on about her business. The old warrior sat down in front of his dwelling and bade the boy do likewise.

"You will be my own," he said. "It is fitting that you be seen with me here before my wickiup that all will know you."

The sun was warm, and it was comfortable there upon the folded sheepskins. After a time Walking Pony dozed. Red Eagle was wide-awake, keeping his face straight and his arms folded across his chest and making no sign or words to those who strolled by and stared curiously at him. Small children began to play around them, and a dog, wearing the pack saddle Apaches place upon them for carrying firewood, drifted up, sniffed about, and eventually followed his squaw mistress off toward the higher hills in search of dry tree limbs.

This all began to grow vaguely familiar to Red Eagle. The children playing about, the thin, starved-looking dogs, the braves sitting before their lodges of animal skins stretched over the three poles that stuck through the top in criss-cross fashion. The smells of piñon and oak and cottonwood smoke drifting about and mingling with those coming from huge kettles of stew brewing over the fires, the squaws going about their labor. The years he had lived with the Underwoods slipped quietly into the background of his mind, and he reverted to those qualities that had never entirely deserted him, and all at once it seemed natural and normal that he should

91

be sitting there in that Apache camp, taking his place among his kind.

A boy, near his age, strolled up and stood for a moment, watching him. Saying nothing, he crossed over and sat down on the sheepskins, and, as a warrior should do, he kept his silence, letting the minutes run on and on. Two of the dogs broke into a fight near the center campfire, and they watched the snarling, tumbling show with interest until one of the squaws came up with a stick and beat the two animals apart. A brave came in, three rabbits slung over his shoulder, and dropped them at the feet of his woman who began at once to skin them and prepare them for the stew. The day's heat began to rise, and high overhead in the clear blue of the sky two buzzard birds soared and dipped on motionless wings.

Red Eagle stirred. The sun's rays were hot, but it would not be fitting to admit it. Old Walking Pony snored and made a strangling noise in his slumber, his head dropped forward on his chest.

"He growls like the fighting dogs," the boy said, breaking his silence.

"Only with greater ferocity," Red Eagle answered, and the two exchanged looks and smiled.

"I am called Little Wolf."

"I am called Red Eagle."

"That I know," said the boy. "I stood near and heard when you talked with Black Cloud. You will be one of us."

"I am happy to be among the Apache people again."

"You came from a far distance," Little Wolf said. "What is it like in faraway places?"

"I lived in a big store of many things with a white-eyes and his woman. They were kind to me. I had many things, but I did not care for them, and many times I would have run away if it had not been for my grandfather friend Cocospero."

"Was he a chief?"

"One time he was so. He was very old and wise, and he talked to me of the Apaches and taught me many things."

"Walking Pony is our teacher. He takes us often and tells us the things we should know and shows us the ways of the mountain lions and the coyotes, and soon he will teach us to be warriors."

"Will he do so for me?" Red Eagle wondered.

"It is likely," Little Wolf replied. "The sun grows hot. Will you not go with me and the others to swim in the stream?"

Red Eagle considered this with fitting gravity. "I will go," he said finally, and the two boys arose and moved through the camp.

They followed a worn path that climbed into the low hills toward the sharp peak that had been Red Eagle's landmark and guide and some time later came upon a small spring-fed stream that rushed noisily down from the higher mountains. Little Wolf turned, and they trotted along the edge of the water, coming eventually to a wide pool that had been created by a line of rocks placed, in dam fashion, across the stream. A half a dozen or more children played about in the pond, but Little Wolf led him to the far side where two other boys of like age sunned themselves on the bank.

"I have brought Red Eagle," Little Wolf said, and dropped down beside them.

The boy felt their eyes run over him, and one, a thin, long-necked youth, said—"The one who talks like a grandfather."—and smiled in a sly sort of way. "Are you an old one turned small or a small one turned old?"

Red Eagle felt a little wave of anger run through him. He immediately disliked this thin one with the small eyes and narrow face, but he made no answer. The other boy smiled up at him.

"I am called White Horse, and he who talks so much is Turkey Neck. Will you not sit with us?"

Turkey Neck sat up in mock surprise. "You would expect this great warrior who traveled many sleeps to sit with us? He is as powerful as the braves! He would have no time for the young boys such as us!"

"Your tongue is as long as your neck," Little Wolf observed, idly flipping pebbles into the water.

"But it talks with true words," Turkey Neck said, looking straight at Red Eagle. "No tall stories come from it."

"I spoke not from a forked tongue," Red Eagle stated.

"Hah!" Turkey Neck cried in high scorn. "Black Cloud may believe such is so, but I do not."

The anger washed through Red Eagle completely, and he felt his muscles flexing, and the urge came over him to take his hands to the thin boy and teach him a thing or two.

"Your tongue wags like the tail of a dog," he said in a low, tight voice, and then waited to see what would happen.

Turkey Neck came slowly to his feet, a smile on his lips, a light dancing in his eyes. "There are things you should know about me," he murmured, and squared his shoulders. He stood almost a full head taller than Red Eagle, but their weights would be nearly the same. "I am the best wrestler, and those are straight words. That you would doubt?"

Red Eagle felt Little Wolf's and White Horse's eyes upon him, speculative and expectant. He said: "Your tongue yet wags like the dog's tail, Turkey Neck!"

He braced himself as Cocospero had taught him, dropping into a crouching squat, his arms half extended before him, hands open and fingers spread. Turkey Neck lunged, and Red Eagle dropped to his knees, catching the boy's wrists as he did so and sending him flying over his head where he landed with a loud grunt in a heap. Little Wolf let out a whoop and rolled away, and White Horse jumped up and began dancing about.

Turkey Neck, quick as a bobcat, came back to his feet and spun. This time he advanced more cautiously, adopting a stance similar to that used by Red Eagle. There was no smile on his face now. He was thoroughly angered, and his pride had suffered a great blow when Red Eagle had tossed him through the air. Some of the smaller children began to gather, hearing the noise, and back up the trail a brave paused to watch.

Turkey Neck rushed in, and Red Eagle side-stepped and extended a foot, and the tall boy went sprawling again. He whirled about and grasped Red Eagle's ankle, and he went down, but he was rolling away as he fell, and he was back on his feet by the time Turkey Neck had gathered himself. They came together, palm to palm, fingers interlocking, and for a long minute they stood thus, straining against each other, their young muscles bulging in their arms and shoulders, legs spread wide, heads bowed. Slowly Turkey Neck began to give, to fall back an inch at a time as Red Eagle's strength began to have its way. And then suddenly Red Eagle dropped to his knees, and once again Turkey Neck soared over him as he executed the trick and caught the thin boy unaware. He had simply let his hands release and ducked out of the way.

Turkey Neck did not rise so quickly this time. He lay flat on his back, sucking for the wind that had gushed from his lungs when he struck. He rolled over to his belly and came slowly to his knees, shaking his head a little to clear it. Raising his eyes, he stared at Red Eagle, a mixture of wonderment and anger in his gaze. He lunged forward again, and Red Eagle stepped away, slapping Turkey Neck smartly on the hind quarters as he went by. The sound cracked loudly, and Little Wolf sent up another laughing shout that was taken up by the small children. Infuriated, Turkey Neck scrambled to his feet and rushed in. Red Eagle caught him by the wrists and fell backward, quickly placing his feet in the tall boy's stomach, and shot him in a long, flat dive into the pool. He met the water with a resounding smack that sent it spraying out in wide sheets from under him, and then he went under.

Shouts and cheers went up from all sides, and Little Wolf ran up and began pounding Red Eagle on the back, but the boy paid no attention. He walked stiffly over to the edge of the pool where Turkey Neck stood, gasping for breath, water running off him in little streams.

"You would question again my words?"

Turkey Neck looked at him with empty eyes. "You speak not with a forked tongue, Red Eagle. We are friends."

"We are friends," Red Eagle murmured, and turned back to Little Wolf and White Horse.

Back up on the trail the brave smiled a little and started for the camp. There was much to this young Apache who had come out of the desert to stay with them, the strength and wisdom of many more summers than he had lived. It was a good sign, and he would tell of it to Black Cloud.

CHAPTER ELEVEN

"THE WAYS OF THE MESCALEROS"

Time slipped swiftly by thereafter. Days in the forests and hills and on the mesas with Walking Pony and the three other boys, and nights in which Red Eagle sat around the great fire and listened to the stories of the men about their raiding and war experiences or the medicine chiefs and the legends of the tribe. It all ran together in one continuous stream, and the years with the Underwoods dropped completely away, and he was truly Apache. The name they had given him was gone, never to be thought of again, and he had no occasion to use the language of the white-eyes, and it, too, fell from him, and he remembered but small amounts of it.

Little Wolf became his best friend with White Horse next and Turkey Neck making a third but not very close member of their quartet, and all learned under patient Walking Pony who regularly took them afield and drilled them with the knowledge all Apaches must have to survive. Theirs was a simple life, and it dealt mostly with essentials which resolved themselves finally into one thing—how to stay alive under any condition. Many of the things taught them by Walking Pony were familiar, and Red Eagle had recollections of times with old Cocospero, but he was eager to learn even more, and he seldom made any mention of such facts but went ahead with his three companions and did as he was told. Often it resulted in his seeming to learn more quickly and with better effect, all of which pleased the old Apache greatly, and once or twice Red Eagle had overheard Walking Pony talking with Black Cloud, one day hearing him say: "Surely the blood of a great chief flows in the body of the small one. He has the eyes of the eagle, the wisdom of the gods, and all are his brothers and walk with him in happiness."

"It is well," Black Cloud had answered in his solemn way. "We have need of great chiefs. Train him well, old brother."

Late that fall the boys were permitted to accompany the men northward on a hunt for winter meat. A large band of antelope had been reported by the scouts, and early one morning they set out, the men riding their wiry ponies, the women and the boys following along on foot. They traveled steadily until the middle of the afternoon when they broke from the mountains and out onto a new land of rolling sand hills and windswept mesas.

"They go there!" Little Wolf exclaimed, and pointed to what appeared to be a long strip of the yellow iron the white-eyes searched for, racing across the prairie in a shimmering band.

"Ah-han-day!" one of the squaws exclaimed.

So far away! Red Eagle echoed the statement in his mind. And running so fast. How would they be able to get close enough for an arrow shot? How could they approach unseen in a land so flat and barren?

Walking Pony rode up on his black and yellow paint horse. He spoke to the squaws who immediately settled down, picketing the mules that dragged the travois, and then came to where the four boys were standing.

"This you will do," he said, not dismounting. "Take this arrow to which I have tied this white cloth. To the top of the faraway hill you will carry it, keeping it well above your head, and, when you are there, you will plant it as a tree upon the highest point. Hide then on the yonder side, taking care that the mesa deer shall not see you."

Little Wolf, who was nearest, accepted the arrow with its square, white flag, and, holding it above him at arm's length, he started for the designated hill, the other boys falling in behind him. Red Eagle had never before been on a hunt such as this, and he watched all things with sharp eyes. The antelope, he saw, had stopped, and the men had turned about on their horses and were deliberately riding off in an opposite direction.

Turkey Neck took his turn at carrying the flag and later Red Eagle with White Horse holding it aloft when they reached the crest of the hill and firmly thrusting it into the loose sand. The antelope had not moved but stood as they had for some time, a long half mile away. The four boys dropped back over the hill and wormed their way to the edge of the slope some yards below. The antelope were yet motionless, and the hunters had dropped entirely from sight somewhere in the south.

"They come not," Turkey Neck observed after an hour had passed, but almost at once the band began drifting toward them, moving a little at a time, stopping and then moving again, their curiosity caught up by the waving patch of white on the hilltop.

Red Eagle watched and wondered. Where were the hunters? The antelope were steadily drawing closer, and he was now able to distinguish their large round eyes, their black horns that lifted straight up and tipped sharply back at the top with but one extending forward prong. The lighter tan bars across their throats and along their cheeks became definite, and one old buck with a night black muzzle pushed suddenly forward and stopped crossways of the advancing herd, checking them while he turned his telescopic eyes upon the attracting flag. The rest waited, heads lifted. The buck watched and stamped his forehoofs impatiently as the cloth stirred and snapped in the light breeze, and then up the slope he turned. *Where are the hunters?* Red Eagle and the boys lay still as quail birds and wondered.

The old buck led his herd straight up the side of the long hill. And then from nowhere, it seemed, hunters raced in on their ponies. They came from behind the hills, from out of the draws, and three, whom the boys had not known were anywhere near, came from a dozen yards back of them. Arrows sped through the air, and the herd milled and churned in confused fright and started back down the slope. Arrows met them there, and they veered again and more arrows came,

99

and Red Eagle could hear the click as wood and horn collided. In few seconds it was over. As many antelope as Red Eagle had fingers lay upon the slope, surprised there in their curiosity by the hunters who had been careful to be seen leaving but who had doubled widely back and approached cautiously from other directions. Red Eagle's eyes followed the remnants of the herd, fleeing northward in a thin line, and he was still watching when the squaws came up with their travois and began skinning and quartering the meat. When they were finished and the travois loaded, there was little left for the coyotes and the buzzard birds that sailed in the clouds. They took even the hides that were thin and of little practical use, but the young girls liked them for they made soft blouses, even though they didn't wear well.

Back in the camp the next morning, Red Eagle asked one question of Walking Pony. "Why do the hunters use not their guns?"

The old chief said: "*Pesh-e-gah* is for fighting and for raiding only. We have but little of the lightning seeds that explode and drive the black iron bullets. It is better to use arrows for hunting."

When the first frost touched the gray hills and stiffened the grass on the mesas, Walking Pony gathered the four boys and took them with him into the deeper cañons. It was to be a lesson in trailing, and this time they would work together. Later, such would be done alone. He stationed them on a flat shelf of rock some two miles from camp, and, advising them to remain there until the sun ball was straight overhead and a stick cast no shadow, he set off through the brush. The boys waited, Turkey Neck dozing in the meantime as he was inclined to do while the others sat and talked of the many things that happened during the summer. At noon they awakened

Turkey Neck and began the trailing, picking it up quickly in the loose dirt at first but losing it almost at once when Walking Pony had swung into the rocks.

It was Turkey Neck who found it, a rock freshly over-turned, and they were off again, moving hurriedly along, watching for more similar sign, for grass that had been stepped on and broken, for a bent branch, for the light mark of a scraping moccasin. Halfway down the mountainside they lost the trail again, and they doubled back to the ledge where they had last had positive evidence, and Red Eagle, recalling his own trick, searched around the shelf until he found where Walking Pony had jumped, and once more they were on trail.

All went smoothly for another hundred yards or less when again the trail disappeared, and they all came to a full halt, unable to continue. They hunted carefully, and again it was Turkey Neck, moving about on his hands and knees, who picked it up, and they found themselves doubling back up the slope where they soon lost all sign in the smooth rocks. Here now was a matter for thought, and Red Eagle ceased looking upon the ground and endeavored to decide in his mind what Walking Pony had done. Sheer walls reared ahead, and it was certain he could not have continued in that direction; thick oak shrubs were to the right, but there were no telltale signs entering them. To the left a huge boulder lay and close inspection revealed no scuff marks upon that surface.

Red Eagle turned and faced thoughtfully back down the trail. After a moment he began retracing their steps, and in a few feet White Horse located a broken twig, and Turkey Leg followed up by picking up moccasin prints, and they moved on to the camp without further trouble.

Walking Pony was pleased with them for they had made good time, and he told them so. It was Turkey Neck who had proved to be the best tracker, but when the old chief had asked—"Who among you found the trail at the foot of the cliff?"—White Horse said: "I found the broken twig, but it was Red Eagle who gave it much thought and retraced your steps."

"It is often so," Walking Pony cautioned them. "An enemy will trick you and hide his trail in many ways. Learn always to think as he does, and he cannot lose you."

CHAPTER TWELVE

"LOH-KA-DIH-NAH-DIDAH-HI"

During the winter months and the early spring, Red Eagle did as the other boys of the camp, hunted small game with snare, fashioned crude weapons with which they practiced, listened to the words of old Walking Pony, and longed for the day that he would be admitted to the ranks of the men. He dreamed often of that, of having his own horse, his own bow and arrows and lance, and perhaps even a gun if he were fortunate enough to get one at some time. As it was, he possessed more than his three friends, still having the knife Cocospero had given him, but it was of little use except for practical purposes, and there was no way he could play at war with it. He did learn to throw it with deadly accuracy, and he spent many hours practicing until it was likely that he was as expert as any of the older men, but he saw no particular value in the accomplishment. He much rather would have had a good bow and a stock of metal-pointed arrows.

The braves did not leave the camp so often during the winter months, and the nights being sharp there was little sitting around the fire, and almost everyone sought the warmness of his wickiup soon after sundown. There were a few raids and brushes with the Mexicans, and once there had been a fierce and hard clash with a wagon train of the *mer-hi-kanos,* and Black Cloud and his braves had been forced to flee, leaving some members of the tribe behind. Not long after that one of the long-bearded white-eyes had come to the camp to talk with the chief, and there was a lot of talk about his bravery in doing so and it was wondered if Black Cloud would permit him to leave. But he did, after a great deal of talk that was held in the chief's wickiup in the presence of several of the old men, including Walking Pony.

That night Walking Pony's squaw, whose name was Flower-That-Grows-In-The-Shadows, questioned him about it, but the old brave shook his head. "Such things are not for woman's ears," he said.

"Will there come more *mer-hi-kanos?*"

"Your nose is long," Walking Pony said. "Such things are no affairs for women."

"I will hear from others," she said. "I would be proud if the true words came from my husband."

The old brave sighed and glanced at Red Eagle, lying upon his bed of skins. Outside the wind whistled a little in its cold passage through the camp, but inside the wickiup, where a small fire burned, it was warm. "The ways of women are a strange and not understandable thing," he said. "The white-eyes is one who has long been our good brother. He is a friend to the Apache people, and he has never spoken with a forked tongue. He came to ask after a white-eye squaw who has been stolen. He would pay the ransom for her. He comes from the *nan-tan* leader of the soldiers."

"There is no white-eyes squaw here," Flower said. "Only are there *nakai-yes* slave women and some of the Pueblo people."

"So told him Black Cloud, and he has gone away."

"Where was this white-eyes squaw that she became lost?"

"On the many-seated wagon that came from the north. There was a raid, and she was taken as prisoner. I would sleep now. Say no more."

"Who would have this white-eyes squaw?" Flower persisted.

"I know not. If I learn, I bring news first to you. Now, let me sleep."

Walking Pony stretched out on his bed, and Flower moved quietly about her work of sewing in the flickering firelight. For the first time in many months Red Eagle thought of the Underwoods.

Spring came and passed, and the grass stood tall in the valleys of the mountains. One bright morning Walking Pony sent Red Eagle to round up the other three boys, and, when they had assembled, they struck out for the high hills, coming near noon time into a wide area where wild wheat was thick and reached almost to a man's chest.

"Here we will play the game of *loh-ka-dih-nah-didah-hi*, and I shall learn which of you has the greater skill. I shall stand near the center, and you will remain here until I give you the signal of the coyote. Only then will you approach, hidden in the grass, and, if I shall see you, I will call your name. It is understood?"

Walking Pony moved off toward the center of the field, and the boys separated, spreading out along the edge. It was something new to Red Eagle, and he thoughtfully studied the land and the tall wheat and wondered how best this game of "he-who-rises-from-the-grass" might be accomplished. He heard the signal from the old brave and saw the other boys drop to their knees and wriggle into the stalks, and he waited a moment, watching their movements, detecting the slight swaying of the wheat's tops as they progressed.

He went then to his own knees and began slowly to work his way along, picking out the small and narrow paths between the stalks, endeavoring to prevent any visible motion overhead. It was a tedious, painstaking task, and a half hour later he heard Walking Pony sing out Turkey Neck's name, and he knew that boy had failed. Almost immediately afterward White Horse was seen by the sharp-eyed old brave, and Red Eagle paused, thinking deeply about the problem.

After a time he resumed but changed his direction and followed out the natural run on the grass, finding it much easier to move between the rows. He continued on, judging his time, until he figured he was somewhere beyond Walking Pony and then turned inward, inching his way with extreme care. Suddenly the old brave's voice said—"Little Wolf, I see your backside."—and the other boys broke into laughter. The sound was very near, so close that Red Eagle caught his breath, not realizing he had crawled such a distance.

"I have not yet seen Red Eagle," Walking Pony said. "Did he not start when you started?"

"I saw him not," Turkey Neck answered.

"He was near to me but, I being busy with myself, did not see him begin," Little Wolf said.

"Perhaps he did not understand and yet awaits," Turkey Neck suggested.

But White Horse said: "He understood well. He is somewhere in the grass."

Red Eagle waited while the minutes dragged by. He was yet unsure of the distance between the others and himself, and he wanted mightily to be very close. The talking ceased, and he crawled more inches.

"Red Eagle, where are you?" Walking Pony called out.

"Here," the boy said, and arose from the stalks of wheat. Ten feet away the old brave and the three boys stood with their backs to him, and at the sound of his voice they all wheeled in surprise and amazement.

"*Ai!*" Walking Pony exclaimed. "I thought not of your coming from behind."

"It was the best way," Red Eagle said, pleased that the old brave was satisfied with him.

"You have much with which to think," Walking Pony said then as they started back through the tall grass. "It is well that you use it, for it is stronger than the arrow or the knife."

On the way back they stopped by the pool where they swam, and Walking Pony showed them which reeds to choose for breathing under water and how to close the nose and keep the eyes open. He helped them locate gourds and hollow them out into a cap for their heads that they might float downstream sometime under the very eyes of an enemy and be unseen. He showed them where they might find edible roots that would keep a man from starving and how to tell which berries were good for the stomach and which were fit only for dyes and paint.

They reached camp at sundown and found that it was being moved. Black Cloud, upon advice of the medicine man, was going farther into the mountains, and the squaws were busy breaking down the wickiups and loading the dogs and mules. In the full darkness they moved away.

CHAPTER THIRTEEN

"CAMP OF THE NAKAI-YES"

They traveled most of that night, the women complaining bitterly at the haste, and, when they came to a halt in a wide and grass-covered clearing near a good stream, it was nearly daylight. The men at once rode off into the hills, and a party was dispatched to observe their old location, many miles to the south and west from where the squaws were now engaged in erecting the wickiups.

Red Eagle and Little Wolf set off together to look over the new country and found it much to their liking, and, when they returned, they reported to Walking Pony that a fine pasture for the horses and mules was to be had in a deep swale not far away.

Food was low, and they spent the afternoon hunting rabbits and other small animals, but that problem was later solved when one of the mules fell and broke a leg and was killed. The animal was skinned and butchered immediately, that meat being a favorite among the Apache people, and, after everyone had eaten heartily and the guards assigned to places around the camp, the usual big fire was built and the warriors and Black Cloud settled themselves with their pipes for the evening.

That night Red Eagle and Little Wolf found a place not far behind Black Cloud. Usually they took only a passing interest in the nightly activities, but there was something in the air, something that had caused their chief to order the camp moved quickly and without delay, and they had wondered about it several times during the hours of the day. They could, of course, have asked Walking Pony or some of the other men, but that would not have been proper; a man learns for himself. Anyway, being such youths, likely they would have been refused any information.

Sitting there with the flames from the fire dancing against the wickiups, they heard Black Cloud order some of the braves to return again to the old camp and remain there until dawn, and to report anything unseemly. The men left, and one of the medicine chiefs came into the circle and began a ritual dance, sprinkling *hod-den-tin* before the braves from the bag of medicine hanging around his neck. It was a powdery substance made of many things, all of which were secret, and the Apache people placed great faith in its magic powers.

"He makes big medicine," Little Wolf whispered.

Red Eagle nodded, listening to the high-pitched, weird chanting that lifted up into the still night and echoed off in the darkness. Black Cloud sat motionless, sucking at his long pipe. The braves that had remained, hunched forward, swayed slightly in rhythm with the tuneless singing, and Walking Pony thumped softly with his fingers upon a deerskin drum. A squaw walked into the circle and tossed an armload of wood upon the fire and turned away as the sparks shot up through the suddenly billowing smoke. The medicine man danced away and came back, a brightly painted stick with fur tassels dangling from them in either hand, and resumed his chant. A brave came in from the shadows, appearing out of nowhere, and moved to Black Cloud's side and whispered something to him. The chief nodded, and the man slipped silently back into the darkness.

The medicine chief droned on for another few minutes and then vanished back into the line of wickiups. The warriors sat up, and another squaw came in bringing wood, but

Black Cloud spoke sharply to her, and she hurried away, not feeding the fire.

"The *nakai-yes* have come to the old camp," Black Cloud said, "and we were not there. It is good medicine we have."

A hubbub of voices lifted, and the chief raised his hand for silence.

"They have many soldiers, but our warriors were unable to tell how many. Nor were they able to hear with their ears the plans that are being made. They understood not their tongue."

The drone of sound began again, and a brave arose and moved to a position before Black Cloud. "I know well the language of the *nakai-yes*," he said. "I will go and listen."

"It is late," the chief murmured. "Their fires will be out, and none will be awake but the guards." The brave moved back to his place in the circle, and Black Cloud spoke again. "It would be well if we knew their strength and thus our attack might better be planned. But our medicine is strong. We shall prevail."

Red Eagle felt a little tremor run through him as an idea came to his mind. He backed silently away from the wickiup, touching Little Wolf lightly upon the arm as he did so. "Come," he whispered, and led his friend well beyond the flare of light. "I would go to the camp of the *nakai-yes*," he said, "and see these things that should be known. It will take short time if we run."

"Let us go," Little Wolf said without a moment's hesitation.

They moved off into the darkness, and, after they were a safe distance from the camp, they broke into a fast trot that carried them along the base of the hills at a pace that ate up distance. Knowing every inch of the ground surrounding the old camp, they approached from a point that they knew would afford them the best concealment. When they were near enough to see the glare of the fires against the rocks, they paused, and Red Eagle said: "Two braves watch the *nakai-yes*. We must not be seen by them."

They turned toward the cliffs after that and worked their way out upon a ledge that permitted them a view of the camp. For an hour they remained there, watching not the cluster of shelters but for the two Apache men they knew were somewhere below them in the thick brush. Sometime near midnight a coyote barked near the north end of the clearing, and at once an answer came from the east.

Immediately Red Eagle and Little Wolf left the shelf, knowing then where the two braves lay, and began a slow, soundless advance upon the camp. It was dark in the thickets, and the moon slid in and out scudding clouds overhead, and there were no noises save the dry clacking of night insects. Red Eagle crawled along a trail he knew as well as the palm of his hand, Little Wolf close behind. He stopped often to listen and wait for a moment, but the path they followed was one used by the rabbits and other small animals, and he felt certain no guard would be near.

They came finally to the edge, and the clearing lay before them. A low fire burned in the center and two men dozed there, their short rifles lying across their knees. Red Eagle let his eyes run over the cloth shelters, making a note of their number. A horse stamped and blew somewhere back of the tents, and, hesitating several more minutes to be sure neither of the guards had awakened, he touched Little Wolf's arm, and they came from the tunnel-like game trail, and, keeping close to the brush along the edge of the clearing, they skirted it to where they could see and count the horses and mules.

It was their plan to return then, but at that moment the sound of voices coming from one of the shelters, placed well toward the center of the group, came to them, and they paused, Red Eagle trying to catch the words and their meaning. But the voices were low, and the words did not come distinctly. The boys waited, measuring their chances. It would be a good thing to hear what was being said, but it would also be a very difficult matter to accomplish. The tent was surrounded by many others, and at any moment the guards might arouse and make their check. Or someone might look from the opening of another shelter, and they would be seen.

"I shall go," Red Eagle whispered, coming to a decision but not wanting Little Wolf to do likewise unless he so wished. "Will you wait at the game trail?"

"I also shall go," Little Wolf answered.

They dropped to their knees and worked their way between the tents, hearing the sounds of men snoring. The moon broke into the open overhead, and the area was at once bathed in its clear, silver light, and they flattened soundlessly to the earth, waiting for it again to go behind a cloud. Over near the fire they could hear one of the guards mumbling as he poked the fire into brightness and tossed more wood upon it. For a moment, Red Eagle was tempted to turn back, but the tent from which the voices came was dead ahead, and, when once again all was shadowed, he moved on, coming to halt when they were immediately next to it.

All was quiet within, and for a moment Red Eagle feared they had come too late and the men had dropped off to sleep, but the voice resumed, speaking the Spanish tongue.

"But if we go from here to the north, we find nothing. These Mescaleros have fled and not to the north. To the south, I am certain. They will find refuge in the Chihuahua Hills and never shall we get them out."

"I know only what the *comandante* said. We leave one hour before sunrise. And to the north. For my own wishes, I would be back in El Paso and not in this accursed land."

"Is it Mangas Coloradas we seek?"

"I know not. All Indians look alike to me, and I know no difference between them."

The conversation then turned to other times and other places, and it meant nothing to Red Eagle. He touched Little Wolf, and they retraced their way through the shelters and to the shadowy blur of brush along the clearing's outer rim. The fire burned brighter now, and there were two more guards, and they paused again, waiting for the firelight to dim, hoping the men would go about their duties. Instead, another pair came up, and the boys fell to wondering how many patrolled the camp and why they had failed to see or hear them. But it was too late to think of that. It was time now that they should be gone, and they bided the moments, awaiting the opportunity that would permit them to reach the game trail.

The moon sailed in and out of darkness. The coyotes barked their high-pitched sounds again, but the *nakai-yes* soldiers stood around the fire. Red Eagle searched the ground for a small stone and, with motions to Little Wolf, half raised and threw the rock to the far side of the camp where it crashed into the side of a tent and thumped to the ground. A cry went up, and the guards wheeled toward it, and in that moment, bending low and keeping as close to the brush as possible, Red Eagle and Little Wolf raced for the trail. They reached it and ducked into its small entrance, hearing the yells of the guards somewhere behind them.

A gun blazed into the night, and a bullet came singing into the thicket over their heads. They had been seen! Red Eagle thought quickly and screamed, the mortally injured cry of a bobcat, crawling away as rapidly as he could. The pounding feet behind them stopped. Red Eagle waited for another shot, breathlessly.

A man's voice said: "Indians! You great fool . . . it was an animal, and you have awakened the whole camp!"

Red Eagle sighed inwardly. They had fallen for the trick. He and Little Wolf hurried on and came out again below the ledge of rock where they looked back to the fire. The guards had again gathered around the fire, and the noise had died away. They turned then for their own encampment and set out at a fast trot, avoiding the sentinels and coming into the cluster of wickiups, finding the fire low and no one awake.

"These things should be told Black Cloud," Little Wolf said in a low voice.

Red Eagle nodded. "Let us first tell Walking Pony."

They hurried to the old brave and roused him. He came to the outside, eyes heavy with sleep, and, when they had finished, he said nothing but took them straight to Black Cloud.

To him Red Eagle recounted the information he had gathered by listening, omitting the incident of the guard shooting at them, and, when he had finished, the tall chief said in his deep, strong voice: "You had no permission to do this, young ones. It is not my wish that our boys place themselves in danger. I am not pleased with you. You will stay with the women in camp for as many sleeps as you have fingers on one hand. Now you will go to your beds."

Red Eagle and Little Wolf turned sadly away, disappointed and crushed by Black Cloud's harsh reprimand. They did not see the faint smile on his lips or hear him say to Walking Pony: "It is good. Your young warriors have done well. We shall greet the *nakai-yes* long before they plan to depart, and our tribe shall be rich with their plunder."

CHAPTER FOURTEEN

"THE HIDDEN TRAIL"

The raid was a great success. The Mexican soldiers were caught completely by surprise and were driven back, and Black Cloud and the warriors returned in mid-morning with many horses and mules, a large amount of food, ammunition, and other supplies, including the cloth tents. But the squaws ignored the purpose for which those latter items had been intended; they immediately fell to converting them into skirts and blouses and other items of wearing apparel and soon were strutting about camp in new finery.

Red Eagle and Little Wolf served out their five-day sentence with much grumbling, but they were secretly proud for the word had leaked out about their part in the affair and few things travel as fast as rumor in an Apache camp. Turkey Neck and White Horse came in for their share of reflected glory, since they were all part of a foursome, and soon it was Turkey Neck who was relating the story of the adventure to the younger children, although he was careful to claim no actual participation in it.

That year passed quickly, and Red Eagle grew tall. By spring he stood a full head higher than Walking Pony, who was of average height for Apache men, and now could actually look down upon Little Wolf and the other boys who were coming along more slowly. He began to feel a little out of place with his friends, and, when fall arrived, he fell to wondering just when that time would come that he could take his place with the men on the hunting and raiding parties. One brisk morning as he and Walking Pony crouched in their wickiup eating, he posed that question to the old brave.

Walking Pony heard the words, but he did not look up, waiting until he had finished, even to licking the ends of his fingers. "You have learned well," he said finally, "and tall and straight have you become. But you are not yet a man. You have yet to reach sixteen summers, and there are other things to be taught."

"It is but soon until I am sixteen summers," Red Eagle said, "and I am large, even as most of the warriors."

Walking Pony in his wise, patient way said: "Do not hurry, my son. Life is long if men be careful and wary, and there are many things of worry. Be content as a boy, for it is but a short period in your summers."

And so Red Eagle continued along with Little Wolf and the others in the endless string of lessons old Walking Pony laid out before them, but an impatience was in him and many times he thought bitterly that he was far from becoming a chief and thus fulfilling Cocospero's prediction.

The tribe wintered on the grassy clearing, but early that next spring Black Cloud moved them back to a place not far from their old camp under the pointed hill. The squaws were not much in favor of this since they had already pretty well stripped the surrounding country of firewood and were forced to go far into the mountains to get their supply. In the late summer, heeding the advice of the medicine man who predicted a severe, cold winter and probably weary of the clamoring women, Black Cloud took his people across the wide mesa to a place near the Rio Grande. It required two full days and a night to accomplish the move, but all were in favor of it, and Walking Pony was particularly pleased. He could now give the boys the lesson that had required strange country as its basis.

Red Eagle and the others knew nothing of this. On the

third day the old brave called them together and told them to be ready to leave camp at sundown. To their questions he made no answer, and they spent several hours wondering what lay in the future for them. Promptly at sundown the old brave and three other men met them at the north edge of the wickiups and then struck out up the river at a fast pace. An hour later they paused, and Walking Pony said: "Here is now a blindfold. You will put it on and see no more until you are told."

"But how can we travel in darkness?" White Horse asked as they tied the strips of thick cloth over their eyes.

Red Eagle felt a strip of rawhide thrust into his hand.

"You will hold this leather and be led. Each of you will be taken into country your eyes have never seen. After which you must find your way to camp by the time when the sun ball makes no shadow."

Red Eagle felt a tug upon the buckskin thong and moved off in obedience. He heard White Horse say—"Farewell, long thin one, fall not on your face in the darkness."—and Turkey Neck's muttered reply—"My feet are not of the thick rocks."—and then he was alone with the brave who walked ahead of him. He did not think it was Walking Pony for the sounds being made were not those of the old brave with whom he had journeyed so many miles and knew so completely.

The path seemed smooth for some distance, and he guessed they were following along the edge of the groves where the mesa began. He let the various odors register upon his nostrils and tried to catalogue them, remembering the smell when they passed through a patch of wild cabbage, the sharp sweetness of a cluster of flowering rose bushes and farther along when the dry tang of piñon assailed him. This confused him some; there should be no piñon along the river, it being found higher up in the hills, and he could yet sense the freshness in the air that would indicate their being near the water.

An hour later they waded across a stream that reached above his knees, and somewhere he could hear water birds making their noisy squawking. They mounted a steep embankment, and he could tell they were then moving across loose sand, such as had been around Underwood's trading post. The quacking of the ducks died out, and once the brave leading him stopped short with a low hiss, and for many minutes they stood in dead silence and listened into the night for some sound that did not come again.

The traveling became difficult. They climbed into a rocky area, and many times he slipped and stumbled and once he fell headlong, bringing to mind the words White Horse had spoken to Turkey Neck, but the brave holding the other end of the buckskin thong made no comment and offered him no aid, and they continued onward. They splashed across another stream, much shallower than the first, and entered into an area that was deep with grass. It was while they were there they heard the screech of a mountain lion over to their right-hand side, and they paused again, dropping to the ground, the brave thinking the big cat might come their way and offer them the chance for a good pelt.

But the lion felt otherwise, and they neither saw nor heard more from it, and once again they were on the move, going at a slow trot across the smooth, pasture-like field. They came into a rocky formation much later, and here the brave spoke his first words.

"It is enough."

Red Eagle felt the strap come loose into his hand and knew the man had released it. He felt around for a place upon which to sit, feeling a little tired from the long, steady traveling under such hindering conditions, and sank down upon the flat surface of a large stone.

"You have seen nothing?"

Red Eagle answered: "My blindfold is tight. I have seen nothing, not even a light streak of the moon."

"Here you will stay until the sun ball rises above the mountains. Only then will you start. It is understood?"

"It is understood," the boy said.

"And by the time of no shadows upon the ground you will be in the camp."

"That I will hope to do."

"Farewell, Red Eagle."

The boy heard him move off, and he sat there trying to pick up the last faint scuffings of his moccasins, but the brave was as quiet as the summer breeze and there was nothing to hear. He felt about the rock and, discovering that it was wide, stretched out, not sleeping but resting his body and letting his leg muscles relax.

Dawn found him thus, and, sitting up, he removed the strip of cloth and looked about. It was an entirely new and strange world with nothing in it that was familiar. He had not the slightest idea of where he was.

CHAPTER FIFTEEN

"DELAY ON THE TRAIL"

There was no green, winding band of the trees marking the river's course; there was no pointed gray hill; there was no wide-reaching mesa, and the sun ball seemed in the direction in which lay the land of the *nakai-yes*—south. He was alone upon a rock-covered hillside, surrounded by short grass plains, and there was nothing to remember. He felt, in those first few minutes, a sag in his self-confidence, and he wondered if, after all, he had learned the many lessons of Walking Pony as well as he should.

He found a small bag lying upon the rock beside him, left by the brave no doubt, and, opening it, he found it filled with strips of dried meat. He had also the buckskin thong and the blindfold cloth and those things, with his knife and the items he wore, were everything in his possession. After he had eaten a little of the jerky, he felt better. He began to think, and, turning about, he climbed to the highest point of the hill and from there looked out over the country with sharp, searching eyes, but he saw nothing that was remembered, and he descended the slope, puzzled but with no fear.

He examined the ground around the base of the rocks for moccasin prints, thinking the knowledge of the direction from which he and the brave had come might be of help, but all marks had been brushed away by the man, and once again he sat down to think. He came eventually to the conclusion that the camp lay somewhere to the east, in the direction of the sun, for, thinking back, it did not seem that they had traveled in that direction during the night. The ground had not risen under his feet, and there had not been enough rocky country. And, if such were true, then ahead would lie the river, and it would be but a matter of deciding the location along its banks where it lay.

He started at a trot, moving straight east, and the going was fairly easy once he had left the rocky hillside behind. He followed down into a shallow valley, topped the opposite side, and found another, much wider and deeper lying before him. He trotted on without hesitation, keeping his gaze moving along the horizon for a familiar sight, but when he had crossed over and reached the crest on the far side, he saw only another broad cañon, rough with heavy growth and rock.

Red Eagle stopped, something telling him he was going deeper into the hills and not toward the river. What caused the feeling he did not know, but it was strong and disturbing, and after a moment he turned away from the sun and doubled back over his own trail. He reached the rock-covered slope and continued on, finding himself an hour later topping out a deep and narrow valley that was studded with small oak trees.

Beyond that lay a wide, grass-covered plateau, and, when he had completed that at his tireless trot and was dropping swiftly down the steep side, he saw far ahead and high in the sky a wedge of geese, and he knew at once that he was right: the river lay somewhere in front of him. He wasted little time after that looking for landmarks. He decided it was most important to reach the river, and from there he would determine his location. He flicked a quick glance at the sun. It was climbing rapidly, and, if he was to reach camp by noon, he would have to make great haste. Accordingly he increased his pace to a run, and an hour later he came out upon a ridge and saw the river lying, shining and green-bordered, far ahead.

At mid-morning he came into the first outcropping of trees, and he paused there to rest for a few minutes. The pace he had maintained was hard and the sun was hot, and he lay down beneath a huge cottonwood, grateful for the shade. It would be easy from this point: he would cross the river, although he could not recall when they had done so during the previous night unless it had been when they were wading and he had heard the ducks, and head straight through for the mesa. Once there, he would see things that would tell him where the camp lay, and he should be able to reach the wickiups well before noon time.

He wondered about Little Wolf and White Horse and Turkey Neck, if they had been as confused as had he. Little Wolf would probably do as he had done, attempt to return by finding his directions and landmarks, and probably White Horse would follow the same method. But not Turkey Neck. He knew that one's trailing abilities well enough to realize that he would find his tracks and follow them back over the exact path that he and the brave who had led him had taken. It might take a bit longer, but for Turkey Neck it was more certain.

Rested, Red Eagle got to his feet and started through the dense grove. Thirst was upon him now, and he moved quickly along, anticipating the pleasantness of a swim as he crossed the river. He gained the bank and looked out over the water, wondering again how they could have waded it unless the brave knew of a much shallower place than he had ever found, and dropped down belly flat upon the grass to drink his fill.

At that exact moment he heard the sound. It was a long groan, as someone in great pain, and he remained perfectly still, his ears straining to hear again. It came and from somewhere back in the grove a dozen yards away. Silent as a night shadow, he came to a crouch and slipped through the brush toward it, wary of some trick. It reached him again, muttering some word that he did not understand, and he located its source—a white-eyes man lying beneath a clump of gooseberry. His shirt front was red and stiff with blood, and his face was ghostly white in the deep gloom of the grove.

Red Eagle did not move. He waited, eyes probing the surrounding brush for other men, but after ten long minutes in which there were no noises except the wounded man's moaning and those of the birds and small animals, he crawled to the gooseberry bush. He was an old white-eyes with long yellow hair and a face covered with whiskers. His clothing was torn to shreds, and the wound in the upper breast was deep and crusted over. He opened his eyes when Red Eagle touched him, and for a fraction of time they sparked with a hope. It died at once.

"Indian!" he groaned. "Might've known a redskin would find me."

The boy stared down at the man. There is neither word for nor understanding of pity in the Apache people, and, as he looked, he had merely a curiosity as to whom the man might be and how he came to be in such a condition. But something also stirred in Red Eagle, something the words, spoken in English, awakened in him.

"If you're goin' to do somethin', why, go ahead and get it over with!" the man said, getting his eyes into focus upon the boy's face. "You sure not takin' me to no camp to get worked over. I'll promise you that!"

Red Eagle searched around in his mind for long, unused words and phrases. "Why you be here?" he said, at last, in a halting English.

The man's eyes widened. "You speak English, redskin?"

"My name is Red Eagle. I not called redskin."

The words were coming back to him now. The wounded man said: "Got shot. One of your *compadres* got a bead on me, but I managed to get away and make it this far. You a Chiricahua?"

"Mescalero."

The man groaned and settled back down, gasping for breath. Red Eagle slipped back to the river, found a gourd and, making a bowl of it, filled it with water and put it to his lips. He drank it all, after which the boy handed him a strip of dried meat. Refilling the gourd, Red Eagle washed the wound, searched about in the grove until he found the proper

122

plant from which he cut the roots and mashed them into a paste, and this he applied as a poultice, binding the injury tightly with a strip torn from the man's shirt.

"You sure don't act like no Mescalero."

Red Eagle failed to understand the meaning. He had done something automatically, as it had been taught him by the Underwoods, and his next thought was concerned with the man's destination.

"Where you go?"

"I was headin' for Padernal."

"Padernal?"

"That's a little town down the way a few miles. You never been there, I reckon. Red Eagle, if you could help me get out on the trail where some of the boys could find me or run down that blamed horse of mine, I'd sure be much obliged to you."

"You got horse here?" Red Eagle said. "Come, I take you."

"You ain't takin' me to your camp, are you?" the man said, suddenly alarmed.

"I take you to trail," the boy said. "You tell me where."

He helped the white-eyes to his feet, but, finding him too weak to stand, he knelt and caught him across his shoulders much as he might carry a deer in from a hunt. The fellow moaned a little but said nothing, and they started back through the grove, in the direction from which Red Eagle had come but a short hour ago. The boy moved slowly, not from the load he bore for the man was not heavy, but because of the thickness of the underbrush, and it took a long time to cover the first mile.

"Where is trail?" Red Eagle asked when they paused for rest.

"Somewheres ahead. Ought to be close now."

Red Eagle took up his load again, and then stopped.

Something moved in the grove. Instinctively he dropped low, and the wounded man, recognizing the furtive action, said nothing for a moment.

"What is it?" he asked after a time.

Red Eagle shook his head. Slipping out from beneath him carefully, he peered through the brush and then turned. "Horse standing in grass."

The man struggled to his feet and followed his gaze. "By George," he whispered, "that's my nag. If you can catch him, I'll be all set."

Red Eagle made no reply but glided off through the brush. In moments he was back, leading the horse. He tied it to a nearby cottonwood and assisted the man into the saddle. When he was firmly seated, his legs tied to the stirrup skirts with leather thongs to prevent any possibility of his falling off should he become weaker, Red Eagle handed him the reins.

"You sure you are a Mescalero?"

The boy nodded, unable to understand why the man continued to doubt it.

"Beats me," the white-eyes said, wagging his head. "But, no matter, if ever you need a friend among the white people, you just call on old John Temple. That's my name, and they all know me around here. You understand? Red Eagle and John Temple good friends, eh?"

Red Eagle smiled faintly. This white man was a funny one; he talked the same things over and over. "We are friends," he said. "Now I go."

He turned back into the grove, abruptly leaving John Temple sitting there on his horse. He heard him say something else, but he wasn't listening. The sun was high overhead and the time when there were no shadows was upon him, and he was miles from the camp.

CHAPTER SIXTEEN

"THE MIDNIGHT COLT"

He swam the river and trotted through the grove to the mesa beyond. He saw nothing that was familiar, and, climbing into the topmost branches of a nearby cottonwood, he finally located the pointed gray hill, many miles to the south, and, knowing then he had but to go downstream until he came to the camp, he slid down the tree and set out at a good trot. Already it was beyond noon time and all hope of being there at the promised hour was gone, but he had good reason for being delayed and Walking Pony would be satisfied.

It came suddenly to him that he could not tell the old brave of John Temple. He could tell no one. There would be no understanding of what he had done, for any Apache would either have taken the white-eyes as prisoner or ended his life where he lay, and from out of the past came a quick and bitter remembrance of two other white men, John-sohn and Glee-sohn, and he had a few moments in which he wondered if he had been right in doing what he had done. They had shown no mercy for the Apache people; why then had he shown mercy to this John Temple? It was not fitting that he should, yet no other thought had entered his mind at the time, and he had gone right along and done what seemed right.

Red Eagle had no way of knowing that the kindness of Amos Underwood and his wife was having its way with him. It lay within him, instilled by their patience and loving care, and it overruled all other inclinations; and the words of old Cocospero, long forgotten by him no doubt, but their meaning firm in his mind—*All white-eyes are not bad, all*

Apaches are not good. It all added into one force, and in such moments it was guiding his thinking, directing his ways and proving once again that as the seedling is bent, so will grow the tree.

No, he could not tell Walking Pony. He could not tell even Little Wolf, his best friend, because he would not be able to understand, either. He jogged tirelessly on, and, when the camp came into sight, near sundown, he had resigned himself to what all others would think: he had gotten lost.

The dogs saw him first and set up their racket, attracting almost everyone in the wickiup village. Little Wolf trotted out to meet him, a question in his eyes, but he said nothing and together they went into the camp and stopped before Walking Pony's shelter.

The old brave was waiting, a frown across his dark colored brow. "The time of no shadows is long passed," he said. "I feared for you."

Red Eagle dropped his gaze to his moccasins. "In this I have failed."

"It seems not easy that you would do so," the old brave said. "You have excelled in many things more difficult than the game of the hidden trail. The others were here well before the final time."

Silence followed, and Red Eagle knew that all awaited his explanation and one must be made. He said: "I was greatly tired. I came to the grove and lay down. I wasted much time there."

For a long minute nothing was heard, and then Turkey Neck burst out with a laugh: "He slept! While the sun was climbing, he slept in the grove!"

The small children began to laugh, too, and several of the braves added their chuckles and sly remarks. He felt Little Wolf's surprised gaze upon him, and Walking Pony, saying

126

no more, wheeled about and strode toward the center fire. Flower-That-Grows-In-The-Shadows murmured in a mocking voice: "He is a wise one, that Red Eagle. He sleeps while others work." The boy turned in to the wickiup. He felt he was a far distance from being a great chief that day.

Such things are forgotten slowly in a system of life where success is considered the greatest of virtues and failure the blackest of degradation, and, as the months wore on, Red Eagle had many occasions during which he had ample time to think about the events along the trail in the grove with John Temple, the white-eyes. Walking Pony never again mentioned the matter nor did any of the boys after a time, but Little Wolf, seeing him in deep study, wondered about it and gave his friend many chances to open his heart, but Red Eagle held his tongue. There was none he might tell the true story to. It was something he scarcely understood himself; how then, could he hope to make others see that what he had done was right?

Late in the month the white-eyes call November, Red Eagle and the other three boys were summoned before Black Cloud. Walking Pony no longer spent time with them, having a new group to tutor, and they had done pretty much as they had pleased in those past days, wandering up and down the river, hunting for small game, trapping the turkey birds in the groves for their tail feathers, and doing all manner of such things for amusement.

The tribe had done well, the raids had prospered, and they were well supplied with all things they desired, and, when they came before their chief, standing in front of his wickiup, he wore a brilliant red blanket thrown across his shoulders that made him appear proud and very fierce.

He let his sharp eyes travel over each boy for a long minute, studying their faces, and then said: "Your time as men will soon come, and you all will take your places with the warriors. It is fitting that you choose now your horses so that they will know you well by the coming of the growing moon."

He paused, and the thrilling meaning of his words ran through the boys. In the spring they would become warriors! They would receive real weapons and learn to use them properly, and they were to get their ponies now. It was the time they had looked forward to and longed for many, many summers.

"With the rising of the sun you will go to the herd and choose your horse. Pick not a young one with weak legs. Nor one that is old and has no speed and short breath. Pick you one that is no longer on this earth than one summer and teach him your ways that he can serve you well."

Black Cloud turned away, and the boys began to talk all at one time. Such a thing was customary among the tribes. A large herd of horses was kept at all times, but each warrior had his own horse and drew upon the reserve stock only if his own became disabled or lost or if there arose a time when there was much riding and his mount became overly tired and unsafe for use.

"Already I have made my choice," White Horse said. "I have seen him before in the pasture . . . a black-and-white one that has great speed."

"Speed is not alone needed," Turkey Neck observed. "A certain step when one rides through rocky country or crosses the river, and deep lungs for long trails."

"You have chosen?" Red Eagle asked.

Turkey Neck shook his head. "I will look for all the day, if need be. Perhaps longer time will be necessary."

"You have a choice?" Little Wolf added.

Red Eagle nodded. "There is a black one. I saw him in the pasture one time. That one I would have if he is still there."

"He is there," Turkey Neck said quickly. "I saw him, running with the others, kicking his heels and biting at their necks. I fear he is of evil turn."

"I could teach him," Red Eagle murmured. "He would be of great speed, and he has a thick chest that can hold much wind, and, if he does not have sure hoofs, he could learn."

"A hard one to catch and teach," Turkey Neck commented. "There are those like him who never become tame."

"I would not want him tame like a travois mule," Red Eagle answered. He turned to Little Wolf. "You have one that is agreeable to your needs?"

Little Wolf shook his head. "I must first look," he said. He could have answered truthfully, saying that he also had watched the midnight black one and wished that it might be his. But Red Eagle desired it, and he was his best friend. Another would do as well.

CHAPTER SEVENTEEN

"THE UNWELCOME VISITOR"

Daylight could not come soon enough for the four boys. Long before the sun's rays were shooting down from the peaks of the eastern hills, they had gathered upon a low knoll overlooking the small valley that formed a natural corral near the grove where the herd was kept. In the gray half light they sat and watched the horses milling slowly about, and at first Red Eagle could not pick out the black yearling, but as the sun rose higher and the shadows lifted, he saw him there and the conviction as to his choice became more definite.

"There is the painted one," White Horse said, and pointed to the black-and-white pony he had spoken of. "I will look no longer. That one is my choice."

Red Eagle and Little Wolf left the knoll, moving around to one side where they might be closer to the black colt. They saw he was strong, that his legs were well-formed, and he had a fine, intelligent head. He watched them as they approached, pawing the ground and throwing his ears forward and backward impatiently, all the time keeping his eyes upon them. Near him stood a rich brown sorrel of similar age, and Little Wolf murmured: "The red one has a fine body."

The boys sat down upon the ground, observing the two ponies carefully, for this was a serious and important matter. These would be the horses that would carry them into raids and upon hunting parties and perhaps war with the *nakai-yes* or unfriendly tribes, and their lives would many times depend upon their strength and speed. Black Cloud would permit them never again to choose from the herd for a mount; they would be expected henceforth to procure their own, and, while those would be thrown into the tribal herd, they would be the ones the boys must use.

They saw White Horse slipping through the horses then, a buckskin thong in his hands. The youth wormed in and out of the animals, always careful to keep hidden from the black-and-white paint pony he sought and finally, after some time, tossed the buckskin around its neck. The pony began to plunge and pull away, but White Horse kept the animal's head low and soon led it to where Red Eagle and Little Wolf sat watching.

"You will teach the paint pony now?" Little Wolf asked.

"I would make friends with him," the boy answered. "My father, Yellow Tail, spoke with me last night and told me of many ways to teach a colt that we might become as brothers."

"I will not do as many," Red Eagle said, "nor break the black one to the post."

"Nor will I," White Horse said.

They spoke of the system used quite often by the men of the tribe in taming a wild horse wherein the animal was staked by short rope to a sturdy post and left in the hot sun for as many as five days. When it was almost wild with thirst, it was taken to water where it drank to a point of bursting and then mounted by the owner; the animal, heavy and logy, could put up little resistance and fight and was soon broken to its master's will. Fortunately this method was used by few men and only those interested in horseflesh as a means of transportation. The animals invariably were stolid old plugs with neither spirit nor sense.

The paint colt, taking a sudden notion to bolt, began rearing and trying to back away once more, but White Horse clung to the buckskin halter, talking softly and soothingly, and after a few moments the pony quieted again.

"How will you teach your animal?" Red Eagle asked.

"I will build a small corral away from the herd where I will keep him. Each day I will bring him grass and lead him to water, and thus he will come to know me as his friend. When it is so that he will come to me, I will teach him to know the weight of a robe upon his back and later will I also be there, and he will not protest so greatly."

"It is a good way," Little Wolf admitted. "I think I shall also do such."

"Have you different thoughts?" White Horse asked Red Eagle.

The boy shook his head. "I have not, and the ways of your father are wise. Shall we not build these corrals near the river, one by the other, that we may help each and our ponies might become good friends, also?"

"That is good," White Horse said. "But first, I will walk and speak for a time with my paint horse."

The boy turned away, leading the pony by short length, and moved slowly along the edge of the herd. The colt fought a little at first but after a few moments settled down to pacing along with his new master. The black and the sorrel had wandered off during the conversation, and Red Eagle and his friend began to search for them anew. They located the pair, still together, on the far side, and, as the boys arose to circle around, Red Eagle said: "Let us get some fresh, sweet grain and give it to them. Perhaps they will then remember."

Down close to the river they found it, and each pulled an armload, after which they returned to the herd and sought out the two yearlings. Red Eagle moved in toward the black that at once came to alert attention, regarding him with bright suspicion as he advanced slowly, talking in a low voice.

"Come, Midnight," he murmured, "you are mine now. You will be my good friend, my brother. You will carry me on your strong back, and I will care for you. I will feed you well and not punish you, and we shall fly over the mesas and the hills like the wind. Midnight . . . your name is Midnight . . . Midnight."

The black pony jerked his head and snorted, backing slowly. Red Eagle held out a handful of grass, but Midnight continued to shy away. The boy kept on, never stopping his flow of words, keeping the sweet-smelling grass extended before him, as close to the horse's flaring nostrils as possible. Finally, unable to stand it longer, the black reared half up and spun around, trotting to the far side of the herd. Red Eagle followed at a slow step, talking in his low tone, and this time Midnight let him approach much closer. But he refused to accept the grass, and after a few moments Red Eagle dropped it to the ground before him and crossed back through the other horses. Looking back once, he saw Midnight lower his head and gather up a mouthful of grass, and then turn to look at him. Red Eagle was pleased for he knew that now the black yearling would thereafter associate him with such fresh, sweet food.

White Horse was still leading the paint around through the herd, having borrowed a handful of grass from Little Wolf who stood with his arm around the neck of his sorrel. The red-toned colt ate calmly from the boy's hand, and Red Eagle was amazed at how quickly his friend had captured the confidence of the pony, but he realized the sorrel was of a different turn of mind than Midnight. He had not the fire in his eyes or the suspicion and would be far less difficult to tame, but likely he would prove less spirited, also, and Red Eagle was not sorry for his choice.

Little Wolf dropped the remainder of the grass in front of the pony, saying—"Eat well, little Firelight. I will see you later."—and came to Red Eagle's side. "You hear what I have named my choice . . . Firelight? He is red like the flames of our campfires and such will suit him well."

Turkey Neck still sat on the knoll, and, when they came to his side, he announced: "I have chosen. See you the long-legged bay-colored one near the center of the herd? That is he, and he shall be called Fast Wind for with such legs he can surely have only the greatest speed."

"What do you name the black-and-white?" Little Wolf asked White Horse as the boy joined them.

"As he is colored, the Painted One," was the reply, and thus the choices were completed and the names given. The boys then told Turkey Neck of their plans to build corrals to which he readily agreed, and they returned to camp for necessary tools after which they trotted to a place in the grove near the river where they built the pens.

They were small, box-shaped affairs, side by side, and were so constructed by a series of poles that one end was left open but could be closed by sliding two bars into place. Late in the day they were finished, and each pulled an armful of grass and placed it on the ground at the closed end of his particular stall.

Next morning, well before sunup, they went to the herd, slipped among the animals until they found their respective ponies, and led them, unwillingly at times, to the corrals. All ate contentedly with the exception of Midnight who still eyed all things with a great deal of suspicion, but he cleaned up the grass, nevertheless, after which all four returned to the herd.

The boys followed this procedure for several days, and then one morning it was not necessary for Turkey Neck to seek out and lead Fast Wind to his stall; he was standing there, awaiting his master's appearance with the grass when they arrived with their armloads. Next day Little Wolf's sorrel had done likewise, and then Red Eagle felt a thrill when Midnight met him a few mornings later. The paint horse needed no invitation, seeing what the other horses were doing, and the boys felt they had accomplished much in their training. The four ponies now expected and awaited them each day at sunrise, and it was time to begin the second part of their education.

It was cloudy that morning as the boys left the camp and started for the corrals. They were forced to forage farther in search of grass, and they came in from the north side of the pole structures, well after the sun had risen and was climbing slowly in a bank of deep gray. Red Eagle was walking slightly ahead of the others, and, as he topped a small hill that lay near the corrals, he came to a stop in surprise.

"They are not there!" he exclaimed.

The others crowded up to him and then hurried to the

pens. They could see none of the ponies, not any of the heads looking toward them expectantly over the smoothly trimmed poles. And then suddenly, from the end stall where Turkey Neck kept his bay, a tawny form leaped, coming up over the top in a smooth, sailing movement.

"Mountain lion!" White Horse cried.

They rushed to Turkey Neck's stall. Lying on the floor, its neck broken, great chunks of flesh ripped and torn from it, was the bay yearling, Fast Wind, victim of the big cat.

For a minute the boys stood paralyzed, the tragedy turning them still and horrified. Turkey Neck found his voice. "I will go to the camp and tell the men," he said.

Red Eagle said: "There is no time. It is we who must follow and kill the lion."

"We have no weapons," White Horse pointed out.

"I have my knife," Red Eagle answered and, stooping down, picked up a short pole an inch or so in diameter. Taking the strip of thin leather worn around his wrist, he bound the knife to the stick, making a crude lance.

"We must hurry," he said in a grim voice, and turned to follow the lion's trail.

CHAPTER EIGHTEEN

"DEATH OF THE KILLER"

For the first hundred yards, it was easy. The big cat had bounded along in ten-foot leaps, and its prints were plainly visible. Soon it reached the grove, however, where the ground was covered with dead leaves and twigs and other trash, and the tracks quickly were lost. Immediately Turkey Neck moved in ahead of Red Eagle, and, dropping to his knees, he began searching for telltale sign.

The lion is a past master at traveling through the forests like a silent shadow, leaving no trail, but Turkey Neck had the sure instincts of a born tracker. In short moments he had picked up the sign again, and they proceeded ahead slowly, the thin youth sometimes on his knees, sometimes bent half over and other times running when he saw evidences of the cat's passage some distance farther along.

Red Eagle followed closely behind, carrying the spear, and the other two boys followed him. Each carried a good-size rock, and none spoke, their hatred showing on their faces as they shared Turkey Neck's grief at his great loss. They went deeper into the grove, the trail leading them in and out of the brush, down small gullies, and once they waded across a small backwater pond from the river where the lion had paused and then leaped across its breadth, impressing his large, round prints in the soft mud of the opposite side.

The cat knew he was being followed and increased his speed, but the boys pressed relentlessly on, knowing that the killer must be removed or he would be back again looking for a new victim. Red Eagle shuddered, thinking of that, of finding Midnight as they had the bay colt, lying beneath the lion's cruel fangs. His sympathy went out to Turkey Neck then, feeling some of the despair that must be in the Indian boy's heart, and he took a firmer grasp upon his improvised lance; they must not let the killer escape.

But Turkey Neck had no intention of letting the lion that had killed his beloved Fast Wind get away. He kept to the faint trail with a cold, calculating interest, and he was never deterred for long by the lion's efforts to lose him. They continued on for the better part of an hour, and soon the lion did as they all knew he would. He forsook the ground and sought safety high in the branches of a cottonwood tree.

"Now," said Red Eagle, "we will end the life of this pony killer."

"You will climb the tree with only your lance?" Little Wolf said.

"I will climb the tree, but you must keep the killer watching you by throwing stones and sticks at him," Red Eagle replied.

He stared up into the tree, and for a minute or two he could not locate the beast, so well hidden was he in the branches. There were no leaves, but he lay flattened out along a limb and partly in a crotch with only a small part of his round, evil head in sight.

"Do not let him leap into the next tree," Red Eagle cautioned as he started up the trunk. "Throw many stones and sticks at him."

"He will not get away," Turkey Neck said in a low, determined voice.

Holding the lance in his left hand, Red Eagle pulled himself up to the first limb. Here he could better see the cat—and the cat saw him and drew back a little, hissing and showing his huge, yellowed fangs. His small ears were plastered back upon his skull, and his eyes were mean, fiery slits. Red Eagle extended the blade of the lance ahead of him, pointing it at the animal, and the cat backed a bit farther and then, wheeling, climbed to the next higher limb.

The boys were keeping a shower of missiles banging into the branches, some of them hitting the lion, but he paid little attention to them, keeping instead his glare upon Red Eagle who climbed relentlessly after him. He stopped again, hissing and growling deeply in his throat and slapped out with one of his powerful front paws, terrible clubs of great strength with flint-sharp claws that could rip and tear with horrible results.

Again he wheeled and slunk upwards to a higher limb. Red Eagle followed, and again they began that odd duel, the Indian boy with his lance, the lion with his forepaw, fencing with one another. A fairly large stone struck the cat, and he momentarily lost balance, one hind leg slipping off the branch, and he scrambled to regain himself. Seizing the opportunity, Red Eagle jabbed hard with the lance, and the blade cut into the animal's shoulder. It brought a scream of rage and pain, and the lion made a short lunge at the boy, but the lance met him, and he drew back, snarling and spitting.

He began to back out upon the limb, and it being small and not strong started to sag. The beast hesitated, looking around, and the rain of stones and sticks from below increased. Red Eagle jabbed and missed, and the lion struck out, hitting the lance and almost knocking it from Red Eagle's grasp, but he clutched it in time. The cat started to inch his way in, realizing he had chosen a branch that would not support his weight. Red Eagle stopped him with the point of his blade, and for a minute they remained that way, the crouched lion facing the lance, his quivering, snarling lips not six inches from the knife's shining edge.

Looking around, Red Eagle saw the cat was at a place where he could make no farther move except downward through the lower limbs or back along the one he had just traversed. To go higher would be impossible since the branches were all smaller yet and would not support him. He was certain the cat would not charge him so long as he held the lance between them.

"Have care!" he called out to the boys below. "I shall use my blade, and perhaps he will fall to the ground. Be ready with rocks and clubs!"

"We are prepared!" Little Wolf replied.

Setting his feet more securely in the crotch in which he was standing, Red Eagle drew back the lance and with a sharp, hard motion stabbed at the lion's eyes. The cat ducked to the side, but the blade slashed into his neck, and he screamed and thrashed about on the branch momentarily as he fought to retain his footing. He did not pause but came around in a wild, furious rush. Red Eagle had a glimpse of the wild, killer eyes and the gaping mouth of sharp teeth, and with the roar of the beast chilling his blood he flung up the spear. It was a quick, desperate move, but it caught the cat full in the mouth, and the beast's own weight drove it deeply into his throat. The shaft upon which the knife was tied snapped like a dry twig, and the beast reared up and backwards and went crashing down through the branches.

Red Eagle heard Turkey Neck shout, and he glanced below to see the beast threshing wildly about, the boys hurling rocks at it, unable to get close enough to the churning tan-and-white figure to use their clubs. When Red Eagle dropped from the lowest branch, the lion was breathing its last.

He removed his knife from the cat's throat and untied the broken length of the shaft and at once began to skin the animal, the others helping him silently. The killer was dead, but that in itself did not bring back to life the bay pony, and they all were sad at its loss.

"He will no more kill our colts and horses," Little Wolf said when they were through with the task.

"Would that we had known of him before he leaped upon poor Fast Wind," Turkey Neck murmured, "but there is one thing that is good. You have a fine lion robe, Red Eagle."

Red Eagle finished wiping his knife and, taking up the skin, handed it to Turkey Neck. "It is yours, my brother," he said. "It is small pay for so fine a pony. Keep it to remember him by."

A look of pleasure and great appreciation passed over the thin boy's face. "It is you I shall remember, good brother," he said softly, "for it was you who killed the fierce lion with your own blade. The prize is yours, but you have given it to me. That I shall not forget."

CHAPTER NINETEEN

"MIDNIGHT—THE PUPIL"

Turkey Neck chose a white yearling that had black feet and stockings and a jagged, irregular blaze down its nose as a replacement for the bay. He named it Snowflake, and, while it came nowhere near to taking the place of the unfortunate Fast Wind, it was a good, strong animal and very intelligent.

But none of the ponies would go near the corrals. Their remembrance of what had taken place there and the odor that yet remained of the lion sent fear running through them, and they flatly refused to have anything to do with the pens. They would, willingly enough, accept the grass from the boys' hands or eat it when it was placed on the ground in front of them but to get them into their pole stalls would have required force, and this Red Eagle and the others dismissed as being a wrong procedure.

Several times, in the days that followed the incident, Red Eagle went alone to the herd, always having with him the bit of grass, difficult to find now that winter had laid its sharp bite across the land. And always Midnight would follow him out of the herd and accept the food, but the incident of the lion had left him wary and a little suspicious. He was appar-

140

ently still associating Red Eagle, the corrals, and the big cat in his mind as somehow connected, and he was not entirely at ease with the boy. Red Eagle set about at once to remedy this, racking his brain for a method that would once again regain the confidence of the black horse.

He began systematic and regular visits to the horses, arranging his appearance so as to be there at about the same time each day. At first he would move slowly through the herd until Midnight was located, after which he would hold out the grass and, with the horse following, lead him to one side. After a few days of this, he took to stopping a few feet away and whistling at the black yearling, attracting his attention, and then walking off. The horse followed.

He pursued this method for a week or more, and then, feeling the importance of the moment, he stopped one day, far back from the herd. He waited for a time until he located Midnight and then sent his whistle reaching out over the horses. For a few minutes nothing happened, and then on the third try he felt a happy thrill run through him as the black horse came trotting to him, head lifted expectantly, ears cocked forward, eager for the grass.

After that it was an usual occurrence, and Red Eagle combed the country for tasty tidbits for Midnight, and it was a simple matter to call him to his side at any time. Thus the establishment of obedience was perfected, but Red Eagle knew such was just the beginning. Many more things lay ahead that must be taught the black one if he was to be all the boy dreamed and hoped for, and chief among them was his acceptance of a rider.

Red Eagle started this in a very simple way. Each time he called Midnight to him and gave him his reward, he would place an arm over the black's neck and stand for a time, leaning against him. This he gradually changed until finally he was leaning heavily against the horse with both arms thrown over his back, half supporting the boy's weight. The temptation was great to climb upon Midnight's strong body at that point, but Red Eagle thrust it aside, and the next time he came he brought with him a small robe of buffalo hide such as was used by the men as a saddle.

When the boy placed this upon Midnight, he wasn't too pleased with it. He waited a little but finally consented to stand still, looking back every now and then at the strange thing that lay across him. Red Eagle renewed the application of his weight, and Midnight soon became accustomed to the robe, and the time came when the boy, by aid of a buckskin rope, left it on him day and night and the horse accepted it as a part of himself.

Next came the application of reins which, in reality, was no more than a buckskin thong looped over the horse's nose and secured about the throat to prevent slippage, the Apache horseman preferring this single-strand type to the two reins used by the *nakai-yes* and the white-eyes. Actually it was used more for training than anything else, for no brave considered his mount completely trained until it could be guided by knee pressures alone. Red Eagle first of all looped the rope about Midnight's neck, and there let it remain, careful that no end should trail that might catch upon something and frighten the horse. Later he added the circle about the black's long nose, permitting that to remain slack, also, and to his delight and surprise Midnight accepted all with good humor.

That he was progressing slowly he was aware. Little Wolf and White Horse were already riding their mounts, at the stage now where they were using their knees instead of the buckskin rein, and several of the braves stopped from time to time and remarked that he was playing too much with the black horse and should have shown him by now who his master was. But Red Eagle would not be hurried. He was still determined not to use force, knowing that Midnight would be a far better animal if he were taught rather than broken to the purpose.

Red Eagle was never to forget that crisp, sharp morning when he climbed, for the first time, upon the black's back. He managed to obtain a small amount of salt from Walking Pony's squaw, and, after Midnight had eaten his bunch of grass, he offered him the salt that he licked at greedily with his lips. While the black was thus occupied, he crawled slowly upon his back, talking softly all the while, making no quick, unexpected moves. When he was seated, his legs wrapped firmly about the horse and had taken up the buckskin thong in his hands, he tugged gently, and Midnight's head came up with a startled jerk.

For a moment Indian boy and horse stared into each other's eyes, and then Midnight began to walk, gradually increasing to a fast trot during which time Red Eagle kept up his slow, soothing words, making no attempt to guide the black but letting him have his way. For several minutes Midnight circled the herd, uncertain apparently in his own mind just what was happening. Red Eagle saw Little Wolf and White Horse come from the camp and stand upon the knoll to watch, and pride surged through him when he saw the admiration in their glances.

When Midnight had trotted all the nervousness from his dark body, he came to a stop, and Red Eagle slid to the ground, still talking and patting the long, powerful neck. He waited a few moments and mounted again, and this time Midnight remained still. Red Eagle clucked to him and touched him gently with his heels, and the black moved forward. They came to the end of the pasture, and Red Eagle pulled on the rein, pressing with one knee to emphasize the requirement. Midnight followed the instruction as if he had been doing it all his life. The boy could have yelled with joy at his success, but he contained himself, confining his enthusiasm to his low, soothing monologue, and, after they had made a few more circuits of the herd, he dismounted, removed the robe, and rewarded Midnight with another bit of salt, releasing him to the herd.

The long weeks of training were about over, and in Red Eagle a happy voice sang. He retired to the hill where Little Wolf and White Horse still stood and watched, and, tossing the buffalo robe to the ground, the three boys dropped upon it.

"The black one is ready?" Little Wolf asked.

"A few more days and I shall remove the halter," Red Eagle answered. "And what of Firelight?"

"He is ready. He liked not the weight of me upon him, but I refused to be dislodged, and now all is well."

"And the Painted One?" Red Eagle said to White Horse.

"As gentle as a squaw's mare," the boy replied. "He knows well his master and does my slightest wish."

"What, then, of Turkey Neck? I have seen little of him and the white one."

Little Wolf pointed toward the camp. "He comes."

Red Eagle lifted his gaze and saw the tall youth astride his mount, racing toward the herd. The horse was trying to buck and twist his rider from his back, but Turkey Neck held firmly, and they came into the pasture at a rush.

"Snowflake takes not gently to his master's thoughts," Little Wolf murmured.

"But he learns," White Horse added, "and soon he will be ready as are we."

Red Eagle looked at his friend inquiringly. "It is not until the growing months that we will go with the men."

"But first we will make our weapons, and for that we are ready. Tomorrow Tall Bear will teach us such."

CHAPTER TWENTY

"WEAPONS OF THE WARRIORS"

Tall Bear was anything but tall. He was, instead, squat and blocky with a powerful body that bore many great scars, and he was a mighty warrior. He had taken part in numerous raids, had proved himself one of the best hunters, and owned seven ponies that attested to his great wealth, but most of all he was an expert in the manufacture and use of the weapons of war. Thus Black Cloud had placed upon him the task of taking the four boys through this final phase of their training.

That next morning he ordered them to procure their horses and then strike out across the mesa. They traveled for some distance until they reached a cactus field, and here Tall Bear showed them a species of the yucca that would afford them the best wood for arrows. Each cut a supply, and they returned to the camp. Leaving the yucca, they went this time to the river and sought out the tree known as Osage orange and from it obtained material for their bows and several long lengths for lances. This took them well into the afternoon, and they spent the balance of that day cutting thin strings of buckskin and sinew for use on the morrow.

It was unnecessary for Tall Bear to summon them to his wickiup. When he arose at sunrise, they were gathered there, waiting, excitement showing on their faces, all eager to get busy at the making of true weapons, vastly different from the crude toys they had once made to play with.

"Take first the wood of the orange," Tall Bear said, when they had seated themselves around him, "of a length from the top of your arm to the ground when you stand. That is of a proper size. Cut it this way." He showed them how to split it and trim it, keeping it full-bodied in the center and tapering toward the ends.

"This can be done quickly," Turkey Neck said, and showed proudly his own completed shaft.

Tall Bear examined it for a moment, held it before him in his hands, bowed it, and it snapped sharply. "It is not so, young son," the battle-scarred old brave said. "What you have done in haste is not good. See, where you have let your blade slip and cut deeply, you have weakened the wood, and, being so, it broke easily. Take you another length and go carefully at your work. Remember this . . . your life many times will depend upon the trustworthiness of your bow."

Saying nothing in reply, Turkey Neck obtained another strip of the orange tree and set about carving his bow. He worked more slowly this time, under the narrow, watchful eyes of Tall Bear, and all were amazed to find, when they finally completed the slim lengths to the brave's satisfaction, that it was nearly dark, and he dismissed them for that day. Red Eagle went at once to the pasture and whistled up Midnight, after which he rode for a short while along the river, glorying in the big black's strength.

Tall Bear next morning showed them how to strengthen their bows by adding layers of sinew, graduated in length and fastened securely together by a glue he manufactured from water and certain other ingredients. The string was next, and they learned how to judge the tension to obtain the greatest flexibility and power. He then permitted them to decorate the bows with painted symbols and bits of feathers or fur. Turkey Neck hung a tuft from the tail of his lion skin upon his as a token of good fortune.

The third lesson covered the all-important arrow. They did not commence immediately to work upon them, Tall Bear showing them first samples from his own quiver, made from the hide of a wildcat.

"Two arrows of different type you will have," he said, "the arrow for hunting and the arrow for war."

He withdrew one from the quiver, a long, slender pale-yellow strip, as straight as a sun's ray and the length of three moccasins. It had an iron point, and three small turkey feathers, stripped from the quill, were bound to its notched end by fine threads of tendon.

"This one for hunting," Tall Bear said. "It must be straight and strong with wood long lying in the sun so that it cannot break when it strikes."

"Do not you use the stone for points?" Red Eagle asked.

"The stone is good but not shaped as easily as the iron hoops of the white-eyes," Tall Bear replied, and the boy recalled seeing in almost every wickiup he had entered during his life in the camp the round bands that had come upon the barrels the white-eyes carried water in. He had often wondered what they were for, and now he knew.

"This arrow is for war," Tall Bear continued. He showed them a shaft of similar length, also with a metal point but so constructed in the pieces that, when embedded within the body of an enemy, it came apart in the center, leaving the lower half. It was made of two lengths, one hollowed out that the other could fit inside.

They spent that day making the shafts, rounding them carefully and learning the method of keeping them straight so that they might fly true and not miss their intended mark.

The next day was spent in cutting out metal points from barrel hoops, which was much easier because one raid had netted an iron cold chisel that replaced the usual sharp rock method. The next day they were shown how to fasten the heads in the slots so that they would be firm, how to notch the ends for the bowstring, and to space properly and bind the strips of feathers into place. Each then identified his arrows by some special mark of design, Red Eagle solving this by dipping the notched end in black dye.

The lance came after that, long twelve-foot poles of slender diameter, made much as arrows would be only with a much larger iron point and not notched at the handle end. There, instead, a strip of feathers was hung as a decoration— and to which would later be added trophies of the hunt or of war. Quivers were then made of deer hide or other available skins, and a week later Tall Bear met them one morning early and took them to a place in the grove where they would practice and become familiar with their weapons.

Targets had been set up at various distances, bits of hide, patches of cloth, wood blocks, and the like, and Tall Bear stood back to watch their first attempt. All went wide of their marks, despite the fact they had grown up and played with simple, similar items, and White Horse skinned the inside of his left wrist badly when he neglected to put on the feather guard that he had made for the purpose. Faults in some of their arrows showed up here, also, and they learned quickly the lesson that all weapons must be thoroughly tested before actual use.

By high noon they had all improved some with Little Wolf proving himself to be the most accurate of the four, but when sundown came, Tall Bear was satisfied. They had all done well, and, when he called them to him, he told them so, adding: "Many times will you stand as you have this day and shoot at a target and then will come that time when you can do this."

The warrior flung up his bow, pulled back the arrow, and let it fly, going in a swift, straight line and striking in the center of the farthest target.

"*Ai!*" Turkey Neck exclaimed. "It is a great distance!"

"As far as a man might run with three breaths," Little Wolf murmured. It was a distance of around five thousand feet.

"Have care with the weapons you make and be patient in learning their good use," Tall Bear said, "and you shall do as I have. But there is a harder task yet."

"What is that?" Red Eagle asked.

"To accomplish this thing from the back of a running horse. Not many times will you stand and shoot your arrow. Often it must be done from behind the neck of your horse, running at great speed. Tomorrow, you will try such."

The boys did try that following day—and with sad results. Seldom did they hit their targets at all, and it was many hours later before they learned to judge the motion of their ponies and the pace at which to travel before they learned at which instant to release their arrows.

Tall Bear gave them their final lesson, almost a full moon, or month, later than the day he had begun. It was in the use of their lances, which, at first were awkward and unwieldy in their hands as they rode at fast pace upon their horses, but as in everything else they learned, and soon they were racing across the mesas and fields, the long, bladed weapons held above their heads in their two hands, charging down upon imaginary enemies. Seeing this, Tall Bear was at last satisfied, and one evening, after they had practiced well, called them to his side.

"There is no more," he said. "I have shown and placed in

your hands the weapons of the warriors. You shall use them well and fear not. Only the *nakai-yes* and the white-eyes have things that are superior, the *pesh-e-gah* rifle and the small gun that can reach a great distance with its death. But by your training you may outwit them in their use. Distance is of little use when they see you not, and the arrow is a swift and deadly messenger."

Red Eagle listened to the words of the old warrior, and his heart quickened. He had now his horse, powerful and wise Midnight; he had now his weapons, his bow and arrows and the long lance. The day was close when he would become a warrior and take his place among the men, and he dreamed that night his old dream of becoming a chief among the Apaches as Cocospero had foretold.

CHAPTER TWENTY-ONE

"THE TIME OF THE GROWING MONTHS"

Many things happened to Red Eagle and his three companions after that day. They found themselves under strict supervision, often by Black Cloud himself, and each morning, when they arose, they found themselves confronted with some new task that must be done.

They were taken to the high mountains once and there left to live by their own wits and devices for seven sleeps. Another time, with the chief in attendance, they were escorted to a deep place in the river and required to swim across and back in the icy cold water. Once they were scattered outside the camp and told to make an entry without being detected by the guards, all failing except Little Wolf who slipped through by a ruse: he remembered that night he and Red Eagle had visited the *nakai-yes* and a rock had been thrown to the far side of their shelters, thus drawing their attention. And always there was the endless practice with bows and arrows.

Near the end they were taken along on four minor raids upon a *nakai-yes* settlement. They were not permitted to bring their weapons or take part in it, being merely stationed at a distance from which point they might watch and see the manner in which such a thing was carried out.

At last the day for which all things had been building arrived, the first day of the growing months, and the boys arose, having by this time a wickiup that they shared, and they prepared themselves for the ceremony and feast they were to participate in. It was their day of coming of age, the time of the warrior, and they hurried to the herd and procured their horses.

Already the squaws had the fires going and pots of stew in the making. Meat barbecued over glowing coals, and the camp took on a festive air as the braves, dressed in their finest and painted in many colors, assembled for the events. The women had donned their decorated deerskin skirts and greased their hair, and the medicine man was already about his business of asking the blessings of their gods upon the great occasion.

The games had started, when the boys returned to camp, and at once they were thrown into the center of all things, foot racing, jumping, hurdling, throwing the lance, wrestling, and similar athletic contests. In all these things the boys proved their abilities, but it was after the time-of-no-shadows that the important tests would come.

It started first with the lances. Red Eagle and the three other boys were lined up on their ponies along with several warriors who desired to try their skill. They held their shafts overhead in their two hands, guiding their horses by knee pressure, while targets were set up for them some distance away. At a given signal all raced forward and hurled their lances—and all went straight and true. Red Eagle was declared the winner for his weapon had driven completely through the target almost at dead center.

The boy was proud as he rode the high-stepping, coal black Midnight back to camp. Many called to him and cheered, and he leaned forward and petted the black's neck. The pains he had taken in training his mount were coming back to him in many ways, and he was happy that he had not become impatient.

That demonstration was followed by a knife-throwing game in which Red Eagle excelled again, although he was defeated by an old brave with four times the experience the boy could boast. After that, the targets were set up again, and they pitted their skill against many braves in launching arrows from the backs of their racing ponies at the marks. They were hopelessly outclassed by the men, but they scored many hits with Little Wolf again proving himself the best of the four boys.

Skilled marksmanship followed that event; small bits of cloth were buried in the sand with no more than a finger's length extending, and riders were required to speed by on their mounts and yank the cloth from the ground. Turkey Neck succeeded as did Red Eagle and Little Wolf, but White Horse, being short and having to lean far over, lost his balance and fell. He was unhurt but greatly disappointed in his failure.

He immediately redeemed himself, however, in the contest of stakes wherein a great number of poles were driven into the ground within a small area, and the riders were told to weave in and out of them at great speed, the object being not to touch any of the stakes. White Horse and his painted pony were the best in this test, which required agility and quick movement, and Red Eagle discovered that speed could be a handicap under certain conditions.

The horse racing was the last thing on the afternoon's program, and, long before it was assembled, much betting took place between the braves who wandered around the ponies, examining them before placing their wagers with their friends. Many stopped to rub appraising hands upon Midnight's shining black coat, and, when at last the contestants lined up at the starting mark, Red Eagle found himself pitted against his three friends and four other braves, one of whom rode a large white stallion with wild eyes and strong legs.

"There is the one we shall have to beat," Red Eagle whispered to Midnight. "He has great strength and wind, like you."

Behind him he could hear the warriors still placing bets, and he heard Black Cloud as he wagered a pony upon the speed of Midnight, and it thrilled him, and he leaned forward again and whispered in the black's ear: "We must win, my brother. Our chief has placed a wager upon your speed. We must not lose!"

The signal was given, and the horsemen lined up in a long, regular string. Little Wolf waved and smiled, and farther along Turkey Neck was having trouble keeping Snowflake quiet. A hush fell over the camp, for such racing was of great importance and always the source of much serious betting. Old Walking Pony stood to one side, his arm upraised, and he repeated again the instructions: they were to race to the oak clump far ahead in the distance and back. The first one to cross the line that he would soon draw upon the ground would be winner.

Red Eagle crouched low upon the big black's muscle-corded neck, his eyes glued to the old warrior's arm. The instant it started to fall he would be off. He waited, and Midnight, sensing the moment, seemed to gather his legs for a great lunge. The arm descended. Red Eagle said—"Go!"—into the black's ear and kicked his heels sharply into Midnight's belly, and the horse leaped forward. The boy rode low on his mount's neck, talking, urging him on. Other riders were all around him, and slightly ahead he could see the white coat of the big stallion. Little Wolf was at his side, and somewhere behind he could hear Turkey Neck's voice shouting at Snowflake.

They approached the oak clump, and a great cloud of dust arose as they wheeled around it. A horse fell, and a man yelled out, but Red Eagle made the turn and found himself alongside the white stallion once more. He crouched lower, pleading with Midnight, and the black kept pace. From the edge of his eye Red Eagle saw another white horse moving up, Snowflake, with Turkey Neck slapping him steadily upon the rump for more speed. The line of waiting people near the camp loomed up ahead, not far.

"Faster, little brother!" he cried into Midnight's slanted ear. "Faster! We must win!"

The black answered the call. His long neck straightened out farther, and his legs began to reach forward, and the ground was a tan blur beneath Red Eagle. Snowflake dropped away, and they were shoulder to shoulder with the stallion. The brave began to slap the white's hindquarters, but Midnight held his pace, and the stallion could not gain.

"Faster, Midnight, faster!" Red Eagle urged.

Slowly the black began to move ahead, an inch at a time. He gained a lead of half a head. The stallion surged up and was even again. Once more Midnight pulled ahead, his great, powerful legs extending far ahead until it seemed to the boy his belly would touch ground, but he kept his precious lead, and, when they thundered over the line, he had increased it a full head's length, and there was no doubt as to the winner.

Red Eagle had never known such happiness. Braves crowded around him, congratulating him, patting his legs and the heaving body of the black horse. Black Cloud came walking through and smiled at him, saying: "You have done well, Red Eagle. The horse you call Midnight has the speed of the sun's light."

The boys rode up to him, and Turkey Neck said, in a marveling voice: "None has such strength and speed as that black one. Snowflake was as standing still!"

Red Eagle sighed and leaned over to whisper to Midnight. "I should call you Great One," he murmured, and the horse showed his appreciation by shaking his long head and blowing loudly.

The crowd drifted away, back toward camp. Red Eagle glanced to the west and turned his horse toward the pasture where the black could feed and rest in his triumph. It was sundown, and the time was at hand for the ceremony.

CHAPTER TWENTY-TWO

"THE TIME OF THE WARRIORS"

Darkness fell. The cooking fires died away, and none, save the large one in the center of the camp, blazed up. Drums began to *thump*, echoing hollowly through the wickiups, and the braves began to assemble, taking their positions around the dancing flames in a wide ring. Black Cloud appeared in his scarlet robe and settled himself in front of his shelter, and this being the signal Walking Pony, followed by the four boys, moved into the range of flaring light and circled behind the warriors, starting a chant that the boys took up.

I am come to the time of the warrior.
I am brave. I am strong. I am wise.
I would ride to the wars with my brothers,
I would be as a man in my tribe.

They completed the circuit several times, and finally Walking Pony came to a stop before the chief and bade the boys to sit, and they did, folding their legs under them, arms crossed over their breasts, looking into the fire.

The drums thudded on. The medicine man came from the shadows and began to dance in and out of the sitting warriors, waving his rattle and plumed stick, ducking and weaving as his songs lifted into the still night air. It was strong medicine, Red Eagle knew, for they were dressed in their ornamented buckskin shirts, and the four-strand cord of great power hung about their necks. *Hod-den-tin* bags were opened, and, each time the medicine man passed the boys, he sprinkled the magic powder upon them, driving away all evil and making them immune to wounds in battle.

Red Eagle felt the rhythmic thumping of the drums seep into him, and like the others he began to sway slightly in unison. The song of the medicine man grew louder as he told of the great deeds of the tribe and its many braves and the chiefs who had led them. No tribe, no enemy, could prevail upon the Mescaleros for their men were the bravest and the wisest and such had been so from the time Unsen had placed them upon this earth as His children. All gods smiled kindly upon the Mescalero people for they were the favored ones. Were not their young men the finest? Were not their fields the greenest so that their horses might be the swiftest and strongest?

Were not their hunts for the antelope the most successful? Did not the mighty Unsen send to them the great herds of buffalo that they might have robes and much meat? Who could say the Mescaleros were not the chosen ones of Unsen, of Holos, and all others?

Several of the braves came to their feet and joined in the dance with the medicine man. Little Wolf arose and followed. And then Turkey Neck. Red Eagle and White Horse, moving as if in a trance, came next, and soon the entire circle had abandoned their positions and all were weaving and spinning about the flame, chanting in low voices. The fire flared up and a shower of sparks descended, but no one noticed. Red Eagle, caught up in the magic of the minutes, was lost in the stories of his ancestors, and, when the drums ceased, he dropped to his place before Black Cloud, breathless and tingling.

The medicine man disappeared, and a brave arose on the far side of the circle and began a recitation of the deeds in which he had participated, carrying on to some length as to his daring. When he finished, another took his place, and a third brave after him until one by one the warriors made known all of the things in which they had excelled and been called upon to exert their strength and wisdom. Red Eagle listened; there were two things he, too, might tell of—the visit to the camp of the *nakai-yes* and the encounter with the lion that had slain Fast Wind, but such would not be fitting. He was young, unproved, and, even though he had accomplished those things, he could not rightfully take his place among the warriors yet and relate the deeds.

157

When the braves had finished, the medicine man came again, dressed differently this time, and took up a position directly behind the boys. He began anew a song, but this one called upon Unsen and all other gods to smile upon the four new warriors and give them great strength and good fortune and protect them in the heat of battle. Then Walking Pony came forward, a feather and skin helmet and a deerskin shield in his hands. He placed the helmet upon Red Eagle's head and the shield in his lap, saying: "Here, now, are your tokens of the warriors. Take them and use them well as you will your weapons."

Turkey Neck's father came next, making a like speech and presentation, and then Little Wolf's and White Horse's parent followed up. It was mere ritual, the warriors having long ago abandoned the use of helmets and shields when they took to fighting from horses, but the tribal custom remained and was always observed.

Black Cloud then came to his feet, a tall, impressive figure in his bright robe. He lifted his hands for complete silence, and the camp fell quiet.

"The gods are good to our people," he said, his deep voice reaching to all points. "We have many good and wise braves, and our young men are strong and willing. Great fortune is ours, and it is many summers since the Mescalero people felt the great hunger or sighed with sickness. It is good. There are among us those who grow old and ride not our horses with the skill and daring that once was within our power. Our young men must come forward and take their places and lead our tribe on to greater riches and strength."

A low murmur ran around the circle of the fire. Was Black Cloud saying a new chief must be chosen? Many shook their heads. It was not so. It could not be so. Black Cloud was a great chief and must so remain. Red Eagle heard the whispering, and a small hope arose in him. Could it be as Cocospero had said? But, no, he was too young, a new warrior who had participated in no raid, no warfare. It could not be he who would be chosen, if Black Cloud laid down his chieftain's feathers.

"Our scouts report a large *conductas* traveling from the south," Black Cloud went on. "There are many wagons and horses. It is guarded well by many soldiers, but we are more in numbers, and with the breaking of the sun's light we will attack. The new warriors will take their places with the braves, and we shall see the rewards of their good training."

Black Cloud turned into his wickiup, signifying the end of the ceremony. The braves arose, and the four boys came to their feet, the thrilling news that they would participate in a raid on the following day racing through them. Red Eagle stood a little to the side, thinking deeply. He was now a warrior, a brave entitled to stand upon a level with all others of the tribe, and unconsciously he squared his shoulders and threw back his head, proud in the realization. He had grown greatly in that past year, and he made a strong figure there in his knee-high moccasins, soft deer-hide breechcloth, and feathered helmet. The fire flickered against his bronze body and glinted off his black eyes, and for a moment he seemed to be looking far off into the distance.

"Would you like to be the chief, my brother?" Little Wolf asked softly from his side.

"I would be, someday," Red Eagle replied in a low voice, and together they walked to their wickiup.

CHAPTER TWENTY-THREE

"CLASH WITH THE NAKAI-YES"

The warriors gathered long before sunrise. Red Eagle and his three companions, getting their ponies from the pasture and collecting their weapons, assembled with the others at the edge of the camp where Black Cloud sat astride his paint awaiting the moment he had designated as the one for departure.

It was yet full dark, and starlight glowed across the low hills and mesas, but the moon had gone, and a man strained to see clearly for any distance. Somewhere in the grove a mockingbird sang as if he might be trying to hurry the coming of day, and far back in the mountains a coyote barked in a long, lonely manner.

"We are ready!" Black Cloud called softly.

A low murmur of agreement rippled through the braves. "Those who ride with the *pesh-e-gahs,*" Black Cloud continued, directing those few who had rifles, "shall be to the front with me. Walking Pony shall be the left wing, Tall Bear shall lead the right."

The chief stopped and rode slowly through the horses to where Red Eagle and the others were. "You shall go with Walking Pony," he said to them. "Have care and watch with eagle eyes, young warriors. The *nakai-yes* shoot straight and well."

Black Cloud turned away and, lifting his hand, signaled the troop forward. They moved off into the semi-darkness at slow pace, making little noise other than the *click* of the horse's hoofs against a stone now and then and the muted creaking of leather, coming from the half dozen saddles that were in use.

"I would get me a fine pony or two this day," Turkey Neck said to Red Eagle.

"Talk not!" Walking Pony hissed, and the young brave fell silent.

A mile or so south of the camp they swung left, going into the hills where they followed out a long, narrow cañon, skirting a low mountain that separated them from the prairie land that lay along the grove's edge. Red Eagle was thinking, not of the raid that lay ahead of him in the hours to come, but of the manner in which Black Cloud was leading his braves; he did not know where the *conductas* of the *nakai-yes* was camped, but he suspected it was somewhere off the lower point of the tall hill they were passing, and he assumed they were making this wide circle in order to approach from the south—the side attack would least be expected from.

They reached the end of the mountain and came to a halt. A brave rode up and talked for a moment with Black Cloud and then moved back into the ranks, and they continued on, keeping to the edge of the hill. Sometime later Black Cloud again called a stop and spoke to a warrior near him who slid from his horse, leaving his bow and quiver, and disappeared into the rocks and brush.

"He goes for the guard," Turkey Neck whispered, guessing at the brave's intentions.

Red Eagle nodded. They must be close now, very close. He cast a glance to the east, estimating how long it would be until daylight and knew it was not far away. The warrior returned and mounted his pony, taking back his weapons from Black Cloud who had held them for him. The chief turned about, and in the gloom Red Eagle saw him make some signal to Tall Bear and Walking Pony, and then the party split into three groups, Tall Bear and some of the braves remaining where they stood, Black Cloud and others moving straight off while old Walking Pony led the rest to the left.

They traveled down a shallow gully that cut back toward the grove, and, when they reached its end, the old brave turned to Red Eagle and said in a low voice: "To the right is the camp of the *nakai-yes*. Get down from your pony and with great care look from the rim of this arroyo. Return and tell me what you see. Have care, the *nakai-yes* have many watchful guards."

Red Eagle, proud to have been selected for this important task, slipped from Midnight's back and wormed his way through the low mesquite and greasewood clumps to the edge of the gully. Taking a small branch of shrubbery, he thrust it into the cloth band that held his hair close to his head and, thus disguised, peered cautiously over the rim. Ahead of him lay the smooth, downgrade slope of the mesa, running toward the grove and the river. Several hundred yards away he saw the *conductas,* clustered in a great circle, a low fire burning in the center. There were a great number of tents like those he had seen once before, and a few figures moved about them. Glancing to the right, he saw a slight motion and recognized it as coming from Tall Bear's party.

Returning to the waiting riders, he related the information to Walking Pony, adding that he had sighted Tall Bear's scout, whereupon the old brave smiled at him and murmured: "Truly, you have the eyes of the eagle, young warrior." He would have much fun with Tall Bear when they returned to camp; he would tell him how the young one had discovered their party and inquire if age was turning him and his braves stiff and awkward like the white-eyes or the *nakai-yes*.

He glanced over his shoulder to the east. "It will be but

short time," he said in a whisper. "We wait here for the signal of Black Cloud."

Red Eagle crouched on Midnight, feeling the strong excitement build up within him. He glanced at his bow, to his quiver of arrows, to the knife hanging by a leather thong at his side. At last he was participating in a raid! Now he was equal to all warriors, about to do as they did, entitled to his share of plunder according to his ability to obtain it. He remembered Turkey Neck's words and decided he, too, would capture a horse that he might have a spare mount. He looked over his shoulder. Little Wolf was beside him, his face tense and set. Next to him was White Horse, and his features, too, showed the pressure of the long moments upon his nerves, and, as Red Eagle looked, he licked his lips. Turkey Neck was on his other flank, murmuring softly into the ear of his white horse Snowflake.

The signal came then, a long, quavering howl. Walking Pony cried—"We go!"—and kicked his mount. The horse shot up from the gully and streaked out across the mesa, and the others followed, eyes intent upon the cluster of wagons. To the right Red Eagle saw another band of riders streaming down upon the camp and recognized Black Cloud, riding well out in front. And farther on Tall Bear and his warriors came out of the broken edges of the mountain and advanced from the third direction.

Gunshots began to break across the quiet. Red Eagle saw the faint orange-colored spots of fire blossom out in the half light near the wagons and knew the guards were shooting their *pesh-e-gahs*. Replies began to come from the men with Black Cloud who had rifles, and Red Eagle saw a horse suddenly go end over end as it stopped a bullet. They were drawing closer, and he could hear the yelling in the camp of the *nakai-yes*.

163

"To the back side!" Walking Pony shouted, and they followed him in a single racing line toward the left, and they became a part of a moving circle of Apache riders sweeping around the wagons.

Red Eagle, watching Walking Pony, held his arrows. It was not yet time to begin shooting. Keeping low on Midnight's back, he thundered along with the others. More shooting came from the far side of the *conductas,* and he wished they would soon be around to that point. They drew in closer, and suddenly the brave riding near him straightened up and fell from his horse, an odd, surprised look on his face. For an instant Red Eagle was amazed. He had been unaware that they were being fired at!

He waited no longer then but began drawing his arrows, shooting them at any slight movement he saw around the wagons. He realized now why Tall Bear had been so insistent in his demand for practice; these targets were even smaller than they had learned with—a patch of shoulder, a helmeted head with only the face showing, a leg or an arm. They swept around to the opposite side. Black Cloud and a dozen warriors had broken through the line of guards and were inside the camp. Unhesitating, Red Eagle plunged in after them, taking up the wild yelling, hearing the others coming behind him.

A soldier raised up in front of him, lifting his rifle, but Midnight's powerful shoulder crashed into him, and he went over backward with a cry. Smoke boiled about him, and the air was filled with arrows and the smell of gunpowder and the noise of explosions. Another man appeared on his left, and he launched an arrow but too quickly, and he missed. The man laughed and fired his handgun, but Red Eagle was ducking away even as the man aimed, and he, too, missed. When Red Eagle looked again, the man was down, an arrow from another warrior in his shoulder.

The camp swarmed with Apaches and *nakai-yes* soldiers and men, some on foot, some yet riding. Red Eagle turned Midnight around and saw Turkey Neck bending double on the back of his white horse, holding to his side. He rode up close and slapped the pony on the rump and sent him trotting from the center of the camp, toward the mesa. Walking Pony rushed by, not seeing him, an arrow drawn in his bow, and he glanced about for a glimpse of Little Wolf or White Horse, but they were nowhere to be seen. He saw Black Cloud then, and his heart almost stopped. The chief sat erect on his horse, head thrown back, and he appeared to be looking out over the battle toward the river far away. A wide red spot was spreading down across his chest. His pony milled about uncertainly, and Red Eagle rode in and turned it about as he had Turkey Neck's and sent it running away from the center of the fight.

Red Eagle charged back into the thick of things, but a strange, fearful thought had crept into his mind. Apaches were falling all around him, and there seemed to be no end of the *nakai-yes*. Had there been a mistake made? Had the scouts reported wrongly as to the strength of the *conductas?* He saw Walking Pony's horse, riderless, run by, and he knew the old brave who had been a father to him was down. And then the black-and-white paint pony of White Horse caught his eye, standing forlornly near one of the wagons, alone. Anger raced through the young warrior. A yell escaped his lips, and he drew back an arrow and searched for a victim upon which to vent his rage.

He saw a movement in one of the wagon beds and spun that way. A woman turned her face to him, eyes wide with fear and horror, her mouth partly open. Red Eagle aimed. But something stayed his hand. Something that came up from the past, reminding him of Mrs. Underwood, echoing the kind things she had done for him. He heard a child crying and the words of old Cocospero, bidding him to follow the reasoning of his heart, trailed through his memory. He lowered the bow and turned away, meeting the puzzled eyes of Little Wolf.

Tall Bear's voice shouted: "Away to the camp!"

Red Eagle wheeled around, obedient to the command. The Apaches who remained astride their ponies began moving toward the mesa, catching up those of their members who were wounded or were without mounts. They maintained a steady fire of arrows as they retreated, holding back the soldiers and the men of the *nakai-yes,* and, when at last they broke out into the open, they urged their horses at great speed toward the protection of the hills.

CHAPTER TWENTY-FOUR

"SURPRISE ATTACK"

Walking Pony did not return. White Horse was gone. Many other warriors were left lying in the camp of the *nakai-yes,* and the wailing of the squaws echoed throughout the wickiups. Black Cloud was badly hurt, a great wound in his body from the passage of a bullet from a gun, and Turkey Neck was suffering from a gunshot wound in his side. The women began at once to prepare their medicines and dress the injuries of all the warriors who required them. The raid had been a complete failure, bordering on the edge of disaster.

Red Eagle stood before the wickiup that had been home to

the young warriors, feeling Little Wolf's gaze upon him.

"My brother," his friend said in a low voice, "I understand not what I saw. I know you not for a coward yet you did as such."

"I could not shoot my arrow," Red Eagle replied in a lost voice.

"There are others who saw and wonder," Little Wolf continued, "and they will think many things."

"I know not why I did so," Red Eagle said. "Inside there was no heart to permit it. I could not shoot."

"But the *nakai-yes* woman was an enemy, even as the *nakai-yes* men. She deserved no more than they."

"That I know, but it came to me there that she harmed me not, or none other. Why, then, should she die?"

"She was of the enemy," Little Wolf reminded him.

"But did we not attack first?"

Little Wolf shook his head, unable to understand the thoughts and the words of his friend. "I fear much will be come of this," he said sadly. "The Apache people and the *nakai-yes* are forever at war. There is no other way."

"There is the way of peace," Red Eagle said, the words coming from him almost unconsciously. "We have lost our good brother, White Horse, and he who was like a father to me, Walking Pony, and many others. Turkey Neck is greatly hurt, and I fear our chief shall die. Would not peace be better than this?"

"It is the way of people," Little Wolf murmured. "It is written that war shall always be in the blood of the Apaches."

"But could not it be different, also? Could not the Apaches live with peace in their camps and harm not the *nakai-yes* and the white-eyes? We need but few things, and these we have now or can get by trading. Should we lose our brothers to death, instead?"

167

"I understand not your words," Little Wolf said. "Perhaps they are good, but I fear they will find no listening ears. Come, let us see how it goes with Black Cloud."

They moved slowly through the confusion of the camp. The wails of the squaws lifted up into the early morning air, and the warriors sat about their small fires in dejected, solemn groups. Tall Bear stood near the wickiup of the chief, and a brave near him looked hard at Red Eagle and spat upon the ground in disgust as the two young warriors came up. They moved inside the shelter where Black Cloud lay upon a pile of skins, his eyes closed, his face thin and drawn.

"The young warriors," he murmured, looking up as they entered. "Where are the other two?"

"White Horse lies dead in the camp of the *nakai-yes*, Turkey Neck is being attended by the women." Little Wolf answered.

Black Cloud stirred. "This day was evil for the Mescaleros," he said. "The gods forsook us in this time. I understand it not."

"We were greatly outnumbered," Red Eagle said.

"Our scouts were good, but they were fooled. The *nakai-yes* awaited us, keeping well hidden their soldiers." He shifted his gaze to Red Eagle. "What you did for me, my brother, was kind, but it would have been better to let me remain and die with my warriors."

"I could not do so, Black Cloud. The tribe has great need of your wisdom and strength."

The chief shook his head. "Against death such things cannot prevail. A new chief must be chosen, for I am not far from the land of many things. Soon I will join my fallen warriors, and a new leader must take my place."

"There are many," Red Eagle said. "Tall Bear and others who may take your place. Fear not for the Mescaleros."

"There are many who are brave and fight well, but few

who have wisdom, young warrior," Black Cloud said, and closed his eyes.

Outside there was a commotion and the low rumble of voices. Tall Bear and several braves crowded in.

"The *nakai-yes* come!" the battle-scarred old warrior said. "Many of their soldiers on horses and many by foot!"

Black Cloud looked about the wickiup, searching the faces of his men with a fading glance. "There is little time. The camp must be moved. The women and children and the sick must be taken away and hidden. Who is to lead?"

No one spoke. Black Cloud's glance came to a stop upon Red Eagle, and he said: "I know well a place in the grove where all might remain unseen."

"The grove!" Tall Bear echoed. "Would it not be better in the hills, in the cañons where there are many caves?"

"Such is true, but the *nakai-yes* will also know of that and, finding us gone, will turn that way to search," said Red Eagle.

Black Cloud smiled. "There speaks your chief, my brothers. Hark well to his words, for he has the wisdom of many. Go now and prepare to leave. Let me remain for I, too, shall be gone when the *nakai-yes* arrive."

Tall Bear stooped swiftly and touched Black Cloud's hand. "I avenge thee, my chief, with many arrows," he said, and wheeled from the wickiup, the others following.

The camp lay quiet with the news of the approaching soldiers, awaiting instructions from their chief. Red Eagle strode into the center, Tall Bear at his right hand, Little Wolf to his left.

"Make ready to travel," Red Eagle called out in a firm voice. "Take food but waste no time on small things."

A grumble lifted from the men, and the squaws waited, hearing the disapproval. Tall Bear stepped before the young warrior.

"Black Cloud has spoken. He bids us listen to the words of Red Eagle, saying they are wise. Do now as he has said for he is our chief in this time."

Red Eagle did not wait to see if the braves followed Tall Bear's instructions. He turned to Little Wolf. "Take you as many men on horses as you have fingers and ride to the mountains. Make a great cloud of dust, as with travois poles, so that the *nakai-yes* may see. When night falls, come to the grove and make our signal."

Little Wolf hurried away. The squaws had acted quickly, and the tribe was collecting near the far end of the camp. They had not attempted to break down their wickiups but were loading the mules and dogs with the few things they felt necessary and were almost ready to travel. Red Eagle moved swiftly back to the shelter of Black Cloud and looked within. The chief opened his eyes and smiled wearily. He lifted a hand in a gesture of farewell and a word passed his lips, but Red Eagle did not hear it, and he turned away sadly.

He whistled for Midnight, and the horse trotted up just as Tall Bear called out—"All are ready."—and he climbed onto the black's strong back and trotted to the head of the column, pointing toward the thickest area of the grove.

A warrior rode up beside him. "Why go we to the trees?" he demanded. "Let us hide in the mountains."

Red Eagle shook his head. "There, also, will go the soldiers, for they will follow Little Wolf and his men. See, the dust arising?"

The brave shifted his glance toward the hills, to the great plume of yellow floating up from the mesa. His eyes came back to Red Eagle, understanding dawning in them. "It is good," he admitted, and cut back with the others, spreading the explanation of the strategy.

CHAPTER TWENTY-FIVE

"CHIEF FROM NECESSITY"

Red Eagle led the Mescalero people in as direct and straight a line as possible to the grove, wishing to get within the thickly growing trees quickly. The camp had not been far distant, and it did not take them long to get there. When they reached the edge of the cottonwoods and the squaws and children and the braves began to fade into its depths, Red Eagle paused and looked back toward the mountains. The dust cloud hung thicker than before, and now another was making its cloudy appearance, farther south, marking the location of the *nakai-yes* soldiers who had turned eastward.

Red Eagle had no thoughts of stopping. He knew there was no safety anywhere within the immediate vicinity of the old camp and that the soldiers, finding themselves duped, would hurry back to the wickiups in the clearing and search for tracks and footprints that would tell them in which direction the Apache people had really gone, a thing they should have done in the first place rather than swinging off from their line of march and endeavoring to intercept a cloud of dust without first making sure.

Red Eagle pushed his people steadily for the entire afternoon, keeping deep in the forest. He roved restlessly back and forth, at times ahead, other times at the rear, and he kept a number of guards flung out from all sides with orders to report anything of unusual character to him. He was anxious to cross the river, feeling that in the steep cañons beyond they would find security, but such a maneuver posed one great question—the river was running high with spring-melted snow water and the squaws and the children and the wounded men would have difficulty in crossing. Yet he felt it must be done, and he watched continually for a place that might offer an easy fording.

Somewhere ahead, he remembered, there was such a place. The brave who had taken him on the test of the lost trail had used it, had taken him across at that point, but that man was no longer in their midst; he was lying back in camp with White Horse and old Walking Pony and the others. Restlessly he rode the banks of the river. It could not be far.

The shadows began to lengthen. The dust clouds in the east disappeared into the hills, and the night birds began to swoop and soar about overhead, seeking insects. The squaws started their complaints, and Tall Bear dropped back to Red Eagle's side, a question on his lips.

"It is much farther? The women are tired, and the sick grow worse from moving."

"We must cross the river," Red Eagle answered. "I search for a place that we might use."

"The river is swift," Tall Bear cautioned, "and it soon becomes night."

"This place I know is wide, and the water loses its depth. There we can cross with no trouble."

"I know not this crossing," Tall Bear said. "You have seen it not long ago?"

Red Eagle said: "With my eyes I have never looked upon it. Once, I waded with one of our braves, but he is not here to guide us."

"Never have you seen it?" Tall Bear repeated in a wondering voice.

Tall Bear fell in behind Midnight, and they wound their way through the trees and brush bordering the stream. They came soon to a long, backwater neck, and here Red Eagle paused, remembrance coming to him. He urged the black out into the water, noticing that it came but shinbone-deep on the horse. When they reached the middle, they found the river had flattened out in this area, and the water, instead of being confined to a narrow channel as it was in most areas, was wide and spread out before them in a great sheet.

"Hold your place," Red Eagle said to the warrior, and touched his heels to Midnight's ribs. The horse moved out into the river, going in a little deeper but not above his knees and in a few breaths they were coming out again into shallowness. Red Eagle turned and rode back.

"Here is that place," he said to Tall Bear. "We shall bring the tribe across it at this point."

Together they passed through the trees and brought the column to the backwater. The squaws protested at having to get wet, but they did not hesitate, knowing well the nearness of danger, and the crossing was made without accident. Red Eagle led them for another hour into the cañons to the west, and then called a halt. He directed them to make night camp and ordered only small fires after which he threw out guards and returned, alone, to the grove to await Little Wolf and the others.

The tribe was safe for a time. Tomorrow, depending upon the movements of the *nakai-yes,* they would either remain here, or he would take them farther toward the north where they would not be found. Red Eagle sighed, thinking of the tension that had been within him during these past hours— and suddenly his thoughts came to a full stop. It dawned upon him that he had been acting as the tribal chief, and they had followed his commands as they would have followed Black Cloud's. True, there had been dissenters, but they quickly had seen the wisdom of his plans and at once had agreed, and there had been no further questioning of him.

He had become chief of the Mescaleros—and still was—but with the coming of the sun a new day would arrive, and a chief would be chosen by the people. Likely an older man, one much versed in warfare as Tall Bear and not one who had lowered his arrow before an enemy woman.

Coming in on the chilly night air, drifted the distant call of a dove bird. That would be Little Wolf, giving the signal. Red Eagle replied and settled back to wait. It would be many minutes before his friend and the braves arrived, time in which to think, and Red Eagle did not wish to have any thoughts. They disturbed him, and many had meanings he did not understand.

CHAPTER TWENTY-SIX

"CHIEF BY CHOICE"

The morning was cold, and the men gathered around small fires and said little. The scouts reported that the *nakai-yes* soldiers had doubled back from the mountains and now were in their abandoned camp, resting there, making no attempt to find and follow the correct trail of the departed Apaches. A meal of rabbits and dried meat was eaten in comparative silence, and, after it was finished, Red Eagle knew the important business was at hand when Tall Bear arose and began to speak.

"Our great chief Black Cloud has gone away, and we have need of another, one brave and wise as was he. I offer myself for this purpose, and all who would follow come stand with me."

174

A few braves got up and walked over to Tall Bear. Little Wolf touched Red Eagle lightly on the arm. "It is for you to speak now, my brother."

Red Eagle stood and glanced about the faces of the men looking up at him. "I would be your chief," he said in a clear voice. "Many summers have I not, but I have learned well, and there are things I would do for my people."

"You have led well," a voice spoke up. "You have fooled the *nakai-yes*, and they know not where we went."

"In the words of Black Cloud, there is much wisdom in Red Eagle," another warrior commented.

Silence hung for a moment, and then a brave came to his feet and crossed over the circle to face Red Eagle. At once he recognized the man who had stood outside Black Cloud's wickiup and spat upon the ground when he had seen him.

"I think this one has the heart of a quail," he stated bluntly. "In the raid upon the *nakai-yes* he did but little, and with my own eyes I saw him raise his arrow to a *nakai-yes* woman and drop it down, not shooting. He fears much, I say."

"This is truth?" Tall Bear asked of Red Eagle in the stunned hush that followed.

Red Eagle felt his hopes sag, and the dreams that had been his faded into dimness. "It is truth," he said. "I loosed not my arrow at the woman for she was no warrior and she had done no harm to me or any other Apache."

"Was she not also the enemy, as any man?" Tall Bear demanded.

"She was a *nakai-yes*," Red Eagle said, "but must all such be our enemy? Would it not be better to be at peace with all people . . . with the *nakai-yes*, the white-eyes?"

"Not so!" Tall Bear roared out. "We shall drive them from our lands, from our hills, and they shall never come again!"

Red Eagle shook his head. Deep and far back in his memory were the words of other men, the things they had said and the truth that had been in them; nothing would stop the white-eyes from coming, nothing would keep the *conductas* from leaving Mexico and bringing *nakai-yes* settlers into the land. Was it not so? Did not the wagon trains continue to come even though the Apache people raided them? Were not there reports of more and more white-eyes along the river? Was it not so that they all increased in numbers while the Indian people grew less?

"I fear the brave Tall Bear speaks without thought," Red Eagle said. "He knows not the ways of the white-eyes and the *nakai-yes* people. It would be well to be at peace with them for they are stronger than we, and we cannot prevail against their might."

"But they are cruel, they despise us, and they seek us not as friends. All are evil," a warrior near Tall Bear said.

"Are there no evil Mescaleros?" Red Eagle countered in a soft voice, and the man became still.

Little Wolf arose and moved to Red Eagle's side. "I stand here," he said, facing the others. "I fear no man, no death, but we fight a useless battle. Red Eagle shows me the way."

Two or three braves came and joined in with him. A low murmur of talk spread through the camp, and several more of the younger warriors sided with Red Eagle.

"A chief of war will I be," Tall Bear said, standing firmly in his beliefs. "There will be raids and much plunder, and we shall be a proud people, bowing our heads to none."

"Surely death and the wailing of the squaws shall ride with you," Red Eagle replied, "for you cannot defeat the *nakai-yes* and the white-eyes. And that day will come when the sun ball shall shine down upon the empty wickiups of the Mescaleros, there being none alive."

At this a dozen men got to their feet and walked to Red Eagle and his small group. Others followed in a quick surge, and the choice was made; a mere half-dozen stood with Tall Bear, all the remainder of the camp with Red Eagle.

"Chief, you now are," Little Wolf murmured, "and for that I am glad. I believe now your words."

The gathering began to break up. Tall Bear strode over, his eyes bright, but he said—"My hand to you I pledge, Chief Red Eagle."—and moved off. Turkey Neck, weak and limping badly, came up and expressed his joy, and then paused as the warning whistle of a guard reached them. All stopped, and many reached for their bows.

Into the clearing walked three white-eyes, one with bound wrists, one wearing a blue-colored uniform with wide hat and yellow scarf and a long knife hanging at his side, and a third that looked sharply around, awakening a vague memory in Red Eagle. The guards marched them before the new chief.

"These we have found coming along the river. We understand them not. They speak only in the tongue of the white-eyes."

The third member of the party, a long-haired man with many whiskers, was staring at him closely. "Say," he said suddenly, "ain't you the Indian that saved my neck here in this grove a long time ago?"

Red Eagle pondered the words, trying to recollect their meaning from his long unused vocabulary of the white-eyes' language. But remembrance of the face came first and a name that was associated with it.

"You John Temple?" he asked.

"That's right! That's right!" the man said. "And your name is Red Eagle, eh? Chief, eh?" He turned to the other men. "We're in luck. This is that Indian I was telling you about. Instead of sticking a knife into my ribs, when he found

177

me, he fixed me up and put me on my horse and sent me on my way."

"He better do the same again," the soldier said, "or he'll find he's gotten hold of a hornets' nest. Lieutenant Emory and the troop are only a day or so behind us."

"Good thing this Indian doesn't savvy English very well," the man with the bound wrists commented. "They don't go for that kind of talk."

"He does savvy," John Temple said, and the soldier paled a little.

Red Eagle listened, the language coming slowly back to him. He looked into John Temple's eyes and said haltingly: "You friend of Red Eagle?"

"I am that," Temple said. "I told you, if you ever needed any favors to call on me. John Temple ain't going back on his word."

"Red Eagle is chief of these Mescaleros. We want to be friends with the white people and the Mexican people. Have peace. No more war. You help?"

"Now there," the soldier said with a slanting look at Temple, "is a smart Indian. Knows when he's licked."

"Indian people not licked," Red Eagle said in quick reply. "Apaches can fight for long time. Many will be killed, but Indians never licked."

"Sergeant," Temple said, "suppose you keep your lip out of this powwow. There's something big going on here, and you don't know how to talk with these Apaches. You just let me do the palaverin'." He turned to Red Eagle. "Now, just what do you want me to help you do, my friend?"

Red Eagle motioned with a broad sweep of his hand to the silent Mescaleros gathered around. "This tribe no more wants war with the white people or the *nakai-yes* from the south."

"Who did he say?" the Army man broke in.

"The Mexicans," interpreted Temple. "He said that in Apache."

Red Eagle waited until they had finished, not liking the way the white man had of breaking in when another was speaking. It was not done in the tribe and considered very bad manners. But the white-eyes were strange in many ways.

"I would go with you to the *nan-tan* of the white people and the Mexican people and tell them so and ask that we go hereafter in peace."

John Temple turned amazed eyes to the soldier. "You hear what he said? He wants to make a peace treaty! I don't know why and I don't care, but Red Eagle," he said, wheeling to the young chief, "you've got yourself a deal. I'll take you to the *nan-tan* of both sides and do your talking for you. I'll see that you're treated right. Man! This is the best thing that has ever happened to this country!"

"When we go?" Red Eagle asked then.

"Why, we can start right now. You can come along with us."

"Where you go?"

"We're headed for El Paso. Got to deliver this prisoner to the Army down there."

Red Eagle glanced at the man with the bound wrists. "Who he?"

John Temple said: "Fellow we been after for quite a spell. Murdered a bunch of Apaches here a few years ago. Name's Gleason. That's the way the white man's law works, Red Eagle . . . never gives up when it starts out looking. . . ."

Temple stopped short, seeing the change pass over the young chief. Red Eagle's eyes hardened, and a spark seemed to glow in their dark depths and his lips became a thin, gray line. A wild fury surged and wheeled inside Red Eagle. Glee-sohn—the murderer of his people, of his father, of all his family! His burning gaze drilled into the man, and John Temple asked: "What's wrong? What's the matter?"

Gleason shrank back under that terrible, hate-filled glare. Red Eagle took a half step forward. Glee-sohn in his grasp, in his hands! He had but to say one word to Tall Bear or Little Wolf or any of the others and death would rain down upon this evil white-eyes, and the vengeance he had sworn would be fulfilled. But that would be the end of peace. The other white-eyes would have to die, too, and with them would go all hopes of making peace for the Mescaleros.

John Temple said again: "What's wrong, Red Eagle? What's the matter?"

"It's some kind of a trick," the soldier said. "Might have known it. Some kind of a trick."

"This man killed my people," Red Eagle said in reply. "This man killed Juan José and my father and many others! He should die!"

John Temple caught on quickly. "I see," he said. "You were one of Juan José's tribe. Well, look, Red Eagle, he is going to die. That's why we're taking him to El Paso. The white man's law is going to hang him for doing that to the Apaches. You understand?"

Red Eagle looked at Temple closely, searching for some evidence that the man spoke truthfully. "The white man's law does not speak with forked tongue?"

"No, sir, not with this jasper. He's going to hang from the highest tree we can find when we get him there. Him and his pal Johnson kicked up enough trouble in this country to last for fifty years, and now there's going to be a settlement."

"The Apache people also have a law," Red Eagle said after a few moments. "It is quick they can settle with such evil ones. Cannot the Apaches do this?"

Gleason shuddered, and Temple smiled wickedly at the prisoner. "I ought to turn you over to them," he said, "and I may have to yet. And it would be no better'n you deserve." He turned back to Red Eagle. "You can't do that," he said, trying to explain in a way the young chief would understand. "You have to let the law do things like that. You want to have peace, but if you go and take the law in your own hands, then you'll have more war. It's up to the white-man's law to take care of scum like this."

"The white man's law will always do this?"

"Always," John Temple said. "You don't have to fight any more. Somebody gives you trouble, you tell the soldiers, and they'll right quick take care of him for you. You don't have to do it yourself."

Red Eagle stood, uncertain and torn by the words of the white man. The strong desire to avenge his people upon the person of this Glee-sohn and not trust the ways of the *mer-hi-kano* moved through him insistently. And just as powerful were his desires for peace and an end to all the killing and death that was shrinking the tribe. He glanced out at the faces of the Mescaleros, watching him intently, none understanding all this talk but knowing it to be of great importance to their young chief and to them. The guards who had captured the three white men were close by, still holding the *pesh-e-gahs* taken from them.

And then a voice seemed to come in from nowhere and speak to him, Cocospero's voice, calm and filled with a vast wisdom, bidding him to heed the words that were in his heart and be a great chief to his people, doing always what was best for them. Slowly he let his eyes travel back to the three men, to Glee-sohn, the hated, evil one, to the soldier with the long knife, and finally to John Temple. "It is good," he murmured. "The white man's law shall have its way. Let us go to the *nan-tan*."

181

ABOUT THE AUTHOR

Ray Hogan was an author who inspired a loyal following over the years since he published his first Western novel, EX-MARSHAL, in 1956. Hogan was born in Willow Springs, Missouri, where his father was town marshal. At five the Hogan family moved to Albuquerque where Ray Hogan lived in the foothills of the Sandia and Manzano mountains. His father was on the Albuquerque police force and, in later years, owned the Overland Hotel. It was while listening to his father and other old-timers tell tales from the past that Ray was inspired to recast these tales in fiction. From the beginning he did exhaustive research into the history and the people of the Old West and the walls of his study were lined with various firearms, spurs, pictures, books, and memorabilia, about all of which he could talk in dramatic detail. "I've attempted to capture the courage and bravery of those men and women that lived out West and the dangers and problems they had to overcome," Hogan once remarked. If his lawmen protagonists seem sometimes larger than life, it is because they are men of integrity, heroes who through grit of character and common sense are able to overcome the obstacles they encounter despite often overwhelming odds. This same grit of character can also be found in Hogan's heroines, and in THE VENGEANCE OF FORTUNA WEST (1983) Hogan wrote a gripping and totally believable account of a woman who takes up the badge and tracks the men who killed her lawman husband by ambush. No less intriguing in her way is Nellie Dupray, convicted of rustling in THE GLORY TRAIL (1978). One of his most popular books, dealing with an earlier period in the West with Kit Carson as its protagonist, is SOLDIER IN BUCKSKIN (Five Star Westerns, 1996). Above all, what is most impressive about Hogan's Western novels is the consistent quality with which each is crafted, the compelling depth of his characters, and his ability to juxtapose the complexities of human conflict into narratives always as intensely interesting as they are emotionally involving. DRIFTER'S END will be his next **Five Star Western**.